Sarah's Bed and Breakfast

by

Dean R. Blanchard

The author has published this work independently, using
the local services of Village Books.

Jacket design by Kate Weisel
Page design by Brendan Clark

Library of Congress Cataloging-in-Publication Data

Blanchard, Dean R.
Sarah's Bed and Breakfast / Dean Blanchard
p. cm.

1. Fiction 2. Novel
I. Title

Library of Congress control number 2018901783

ISBN 978-0-9862-0432-6

This is a work of fiction.
Names, characters, places, and incidents are either the
product of the author's imagination, or used fictitiously.
Any resemblance to actual persons, living or dead,
events, or locales is entirely coincidental.

Printed in the United States of America
First Edition

Dedication

For my beloved daughter, Malisa, and my twin sons,

Jason Dean and Justin Drew

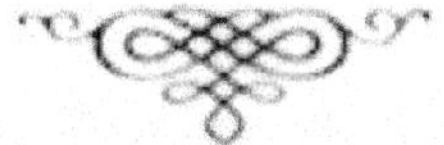

Cast of Characters

Beulah Anderson – Owner of Sarah's Bed and Breakfast
Miriam Covington – Luke Covington's widow
Tyler Moore – Miriam's second husband
Ethan Covington – Sarah's only son
Jake Covington – Miriam's adopted son
Tony Wong – Beulah's soul mate
Margo Wong – Tony's daughter
Elsa Meyers – Historical Society
Gary Souls – *Covington Banner* Publisher
Heather Souls – Gary's wife, reporter, photographer
Patricia Marr – Friend of Heather Souls
Bud Silverman – Navy Recruiter

Table of Contents

Chapter 1

Soon after Beulah Anderson opened Sarah's Bed and Breakfast, she decided to investigate the dilapidated garage to see if there were any items of value. The pungent odor of mold and mildew so filled the air that Beulah started to leave. It was then that she caught sight of an object that sat on top of a workbench that was cobwebbed with an assortment of carpentry items. When she got a closer look at the object, she discovered that it was a metal box.

With her fingers, she picked up the metal box and as she did, a fine layer of dust that covered the metal box exploded into the air. She fanned the air around her face with her hand. After a few moments, the dust settled and then she took the metal box into the kitchen and had set it next to the kitchen sink to clean it off when Tony Wong and Ethan, Sarah Covington's only son, arrived to tear down the garage. Tony poured two cups of coffee, one for himself and one for Ethan. They walked over to Beulah and looked over her shoulder.

Ethan asked, "Where did you find this box?"

"Out in the garage," Beulah said. She removed a blackened towel and detergent from under the sink. She held the metal box over the kitchen sink as she sprayed the box with detergent and then rinsed and wiped the box clean. It was then she noticed a name written in red: *Rose C.*

Beulah had a junk drawer at the bottom of the kitchen counter. She opened the drawer and removed a hammer. When she hit the metal box with the hammer, the lid fell off because the hinges of the box were rusted. Ethan and Tony stood behind her and looked over her shoulder to see what was in the metal box. They saw several small, discolored photographs taken with a Kodak Brownie camera along with a piece of yellowed note paper that read, *I will never forgive you.*

Thinking aloud Ethan asked, "Rose C? Was she a Covington?"

"I have no idea," Beulah said.

She put all the items back inside the metal box and soon after that she looked at Tony and said, "I sure would like to know what this is all about."

Tony suggested, "Why don't you put it on the fireplace mantel—a great mystery of ours." Beulah thought a lot about the metal box the rest of the day.

In the meantime, Ethan helped Tony raze the dilapidated garage. Tony hooked up a come-along to his pickup and fastened a steel wire to one corner of the garage. With just one pull on the steel wire, the building collapsed to the ground, sending pungent dirt in all directions.

Tony drove the sagging pickup to a landfill where he and Ethan dumped the remains of the garage.

Beulah sketched plans to construct a new garage with a studio apartment above it. This would be her own residence. Tony had gone to the lumberyard and purchased cedar boards and the other required materials.

He built a covered staircase from the studio apartment down to the main floor of Sarah's Bed and Breakfast that opened to the back of the building, adjacent to the back door. It was a timely decision because business had increased at the Bed and Breakfast to the point where Beulah needed to put in many hours each day managing the business.

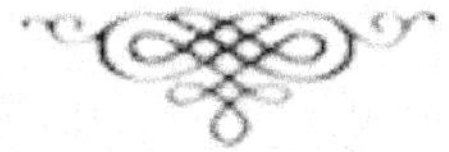

Chapter 2

At times when Beulah could slip away from Sarah's Bed and Breakfast, she would explore antique shops, flea markets, and garage sales. This is how Beulah found pictures, pillows, bed sheets, and some knickknacks she would use in Sarah's Bed and Breakfast. She took Ethan and Margo, Tony's daughter, with her whenever the three of them could get together. Beulah knew the difference between an antique and a piece of junk.

The highlight of one of her shopping sprees came about when Beulah found a multicolored tablecloth and a twelve-piece setting of Fiesta ware made by Homer Laughlin, complete with drinking glasses.

Ethan had gifted Beulah with his mom's china. Each plate had a Fluffy Rose with the Homer Laughlin seal on the back. He also gave Beulah his mom's wedding tablecloth with a faded whiskey spill on one corner, along with her wedding flatware, American Harmony by Oneida—all these were gifts that his mom and dad received from their grange families on the day of their wedding.

Beulah bought a china hutch with etched glass doors that had a light inside it. She put all of Sarah's china and flatware in the hutch. In one long drawer Beulah placed the linen tablecloth with the faded whiskey stain on one corner. That tablecloth would become the topic of many conversations in Sarah's Bed and Breakfast.

For the first year after Sarah's death, Beulah wept at her memories of Sarah each time she held one of those dishes. Eventually she remembered what she told Sarah the first time Sarah showed her the priceless wedding gifts. They were stored in a cardboard box in Sarah's bedroom because she was protecting them from the damage of everyday use.

Beulah remembered telling Sarah, "Andrew wouldn't want these beautiful wedding gifts hidden from view."

Chapter 3

Covington town has a variety of cemeteries, one each for Catholics, Jews, Mormons, Methodists, Dutch, Protestants, and Chinese. The poverty-stricken and those who had no known family ties to anyone in the town were buried in a cemetery on the south side of town where weeds choked the cemetery grounds.

Beulah sat on a wooden bench at the graveside where Sarah and Andrew Covington lay. It was a mild summer afternoon. The smell of newly mowed grass filled the air. Small American flags were positioned in front of all the grave markers. In the distance, she saw a riding lawnmower winding its way through the cemetery. She turned her attention to the grave marker. She ran the tips of her fingers over the etched lettering on the tombstone and as she did this, she heard the muffled conversations between people in the distance behind her. When she turned, she saw uniformed soldiers standing at attention. What she saw next shook her to the core. One of the soldiers gave the American flag to a woman dressed in black. The woman pulled back the black scarf that covered her face and when she did Beulah saw herself as that woman.

In that awful moment, Beulah realized that the grave marker was for Lloyd Covington, her husband. He had trained to become a fighter pilot at the naval air station in San Diego, California. During one of his training missions, he lost control of his plane. The jet rolled over on its back as it crashed onto the tarmac close to the air control tower. The explosion shattered glass in the control tower's windows and windows throughout the base. The explosion shook the ground so hard that some base personnel thought they had just felt a small earthquake.

Lloyd Covington was given a military gravesite ceremony complete with taps and gun salute. He was buried at Fort Rosecrans National Cemetery. Beulah's father was a nurturing man while her mother, a German woman, stood stern-faced throughout the ceremony. Beulah knew that her mother did not show much affection yet she was sure that her mother loved her.

Beulah had managed the officers' club on the naval base in San Diego. Before she married Lloyd, she had graduated from a local university with a degree in accounting. A month after her husband's death and burial, Beulah found a small blurb in the local newspaper advertising for an experienced accountant in a place called Covington, Iowa. An accounting firm, listing a telephone number and the name Luke Covington, proprietor, was looking for an experienced accountant, preferably a woman.

Beulah was ready to move away from San Diego, from all her well-meaning friends who wanted to introduce Beulah to single Marines they believed were a lot like Lloyd.

Beulah answered the ad and moved to the town of Covington, Iowa, believing that this Luke Covington would be of the same gentle character as her husband, Lloyd Covington. Within one week at Luke's accounting business, Beulah realized Luke was nothing like her husband, Lloyd.

A brief time later at a local grange dance, Beulah met Sarah and Andrew Covington. She also met Luke's wife, Miriam. Beulah soon discovered that Luke and Miriam were not the happy couple they pretended to be.

Miriam had no sense of makeup; her lips were smeared with red lipstick and her cheeks were plastered in rouge. She talked about how she and Luke were in love while they pretended affection. Beulah knew what a deep, abiding love and friendship was all about. She and Lloyd were best friends first and then they fell in love.

Beulah's friendship with Sarah blossomed immediately because for Beulah, Sarah was the sister she always wished she had. She was a kind, gentle soul who had a son, Ethan. He was a mirror image of Andrew, his father, so Sarah told Beulah.

Beulah snapped straight up on the edge of her bed as shock turned to horror. She wrapped her arms round her chest and then she stood up, wobbly at first. Her vision blurred momentarily as she wiped her eyes clear with her fingertips. She walked out of her bedroom and down the staircase leading into the kitchen. She made a pot of coffee and poured herself a cup. She sat at the breakfast nook through daybreak. Her hands were wrapped around the hot cup. She sat numb for several moments. Eventually she leaned back and gazed out of the window over the front yard that was covered with a foot of new snow. Suddenly two deer, a doe and a fawn, came into the yard. They stopped and looked at the breakfast nook window as if they sensed Beulah looking out at them. The deer were a beautiful sight to Beulah, and in that moment, she temporarily forgot the horrible dream. The deer and Beulah stared at each other for the longest time before finally they pranced out of the yard.

Beulah glanced at the clock that hung on the wall above the kitchen sink. It was 6 a.m. Exhausted, she rested her head on the breakfast nook table, closed her eyes, and faded into a slumber. She was awakened when the back door opened. When Tony walked into the kitchen, Beulah sprang to her feet and threw herself into his arms, crying aloud. Her body trembled to the point where Tony held onto her tightly and then he looked at her and asked, "What happened?"

Beulah responded, her voice shaking, "I dreamt that I was sitting in front of Lloyd's grave marker. I remember when Lloyd's plane crashed. I got sick to my stomach. I just knew in the pit of my heart that Lloyd had died because I felt his spirit pass through me."

Tony guided her into the breakfast nook. He slid into the bench next to her. He looked at Beulah with tears in his eyes and said, "I know I will never be able to replace Lloyd, and I've never tried to take Lloyd's place in your life but I do love you, Beulah."

Beulah hugged Tony close to her. She kissed his forehead and then looked at him and said, "I'm not asking you to replace Lloyd." She loved Tony because he was a loving, caring man. She paused momentarily, struggling with her emotions. "I get so tired sometimes. I wonder if I did the right thing by opening the Bed and Breakfast. Margo and Ethan do a lot of work for me. They never complain."

Tony asked, "What was the name of that cleaning business you had?"

"The business you set me up with?" she paused. "Two Hens and a Rooster."

Tony nodded. "Are they still in business?"

"I need to get my telephone book."

"I'll get it for you."

Beulah gestured towards the counter across from the breakfast nook when she said, "The telephone is on top of it."

Tony brought the telephone and the book to Beulah and sat down next to her. Beulah opened the telephone book to the yellow pages and looked at advertisements for housecleaning businesses. It was then she noticed an ad for Two Hens and a Rooster.

When Beulah dialed the telephone number, she heard a woman's voice, "Tucker's residence." Beulah hesitated for a moment because she could not remember their names.

"This is Beulah Anderson."

"A voice from our past! How are you doing?"

Tony squeezed Beulah's hand as he whispered, "I've work to do."

"Love you," Beulah said as she kissed him. Beulah admitted after Tony left, "I'm terrible at names."

"Beverly and Franklin. You set us up in a housecleaning business. How are you doing?"

"I am well, thank you for asking. Are you and Franklin still in the housecleaning work?" Beulah asked.

"We don't clean houses any more. Franklin slipped and fell on the sidewalk outside our home. He's in bad shape, so I spend a lot of time taking care of him."

"Our son, Joseph, is on active duty with the Air Force. He flies jets! He's about to retire. He got his commercial pilot's license while he was in the Air Force." She paused briefly. "He got a job flying for a mail carrier. We're so excited for him. He bought a home in Des Moines. After he and his family are settled into their new home, Franklin and I will be moving there.

Joseph bought a home that has a mother-in-law apartment next to his home. Weren't you married at one time?" Beverly asked.

Beulah told Beverly about her father in the Marines and her husband being a Navy pilot.

Beverly asked, "Did your husband retire out of the military?"

Sadly, Beulah said, "No, he was killed during a training accident."

"Oh my," Beverly said. "What are you doing now?"

"I run Sarah's Bed and Breakfast. Why don't you and Franklin come over for coffee tomorrow at noon?"

"We'll be there."

After Beulah hung up the receiver, Tony came back into the Bed and Breakfast and sat down at the breakfast nook.

"There's a tingling in my left leg," he said as he massaged the leg with his hands.

"How long has the tingling been going on?" Beulah asked.

"The numbness just started," Tony said.

"Maybe I should take you to the hospital to get it checked out."

"It's my leg, not my heart."

Beulah looked at him and said, "Help me get this place ready for when Beverly and Franklin come over tomorrow."

"What's wrong with the way it looks now?" Tony asked.

"There's a lot of dusting, the upstairs bedrooms need to be gone over and the bathrooms, too," she paused. "I need to bake some banana-walnut muffins while you dust. I'll take care of the upstairs." After Beulah made the muffins and put them into the oven, she set the timer on the stove.

Half an hour passed when Tony's left leg gave out and he had to sit down on the davenport. When the pain radiated down his left leg, he called out to Beulah, "I need you!"

Just as Beulah came running down the steps, the timer to the oven went off. She raced into the kitchen, removed the muffins from the oven, and set them on top of the counter next to the stove. She turned the oven off and then went back into the living room. "Let's get you to the hospital," she insisted.

"We'll go tomorrow after they leave. I can wait that long."

She knew there was something going on with Tony when she saw him massage his left leg, then his left arm and his neck, and suddenly he had a shortness of breath.

Tony said in a calm voice, "We'll go tomorrow afternoon after they are gone."

The following day at noon Beulah had set out the banana-walnut muffins on the breakfast nook table. Tony made a pot of coffee and set creamer and sugar on the breakfast nook table.

The noon hour came. They waited half an hour more, just to be sure.

They never came.

That night Beulah did not get much sleep because Tony's body radiated heat. He sweat. His skin felt cold and clammy when she touched him and his hair was soaked from his perspiration.

It was in the early morning hours when Tony got out of bed to go to the bathroom. As he stood up he landed on the floor with a dull thud.

Beulah shot up out of bed and ran over to him. When she held him in her arms she noticed his eyes showed no sign of life.

In a burst of adrenaline, Beulah lifted Tony back onto the bed. She tumbled over his body to get to the telephone that was on the nightstand on the other side of the bed. Her hands shook as she dialed the number for the hospital and then the Peking Duck where Margo slept. As soon as Margo picked up the receiver Beulah said, "Your dad has had a stroke. The ambulance is on its way. You need to get ahold of Ethan."

Soon the ambulance arrived to take Tony to the hospital. Beulah was in shock when she arrived at the hospital along with Margo and Ethan. Ethan and Margo ran ahead towards the emergency room where Tony lay.

Exhausted and drained of energy, Beulah found her way to Tony's room. She tried to stay calm as the doctor with the help of a nurse examined Tony. The doctor took his blood pressure and placed his stethoscope to Tony's chest and around his back.

"What has happened to him?" Margo asked. She sat in stunned fear; her father had been her lifelong best friend until she met Ethan.

After the doctor completed his examination, he lay the stethoscope around his neck. He checked Tony's pulse and then looked at Margo. "Your father has heart disease. He has an irregular heart beat and coupled with high blood pressure, he's a candidate for stroke. Did you bring him in?"

"Beulah did," Margo said as she pointed to Beulah.

The doctor said, "He wouldn't have lasted another day. It's a wonder he hasn't had a stroke before now." The doctor warned Tony, "Your next stroke, you'll meet the grim reaper."

Tony suddenly became aware of where he was and started to get out of his bed.

Margo grabbed his arm.

"Dad, you had a stroke!"

Tony looked at the doctor and asked, "Are you done with me?"

Reluctantly the doctor said, "I am, but you need to take better care of yourself."

Tony sat on the edge of his bed to get up. He brought Margo close to him. She sobbed into his shoulder.

Ethan held Margo close to his side as he looked at Tony and said, "Things wouldn't be the same around here without you in our lives."

"Let's go home," Tony said as he stood up to leave.

Beulah hugged Tony close to her as she cried aloud, "You gave me quite a scare."

Tony kissed Beulah and then said "I scared me, too. I'll take better care of myself."

He never did.

Chapter 4

A month after Tony's stroke, Beulah recalled when she bought the house from Miriam. When Luke, Miriam's husband died, he left Miriam penniless. Miriam had located a file in Luke's office, after his funeral, that showed he had been sending money to a woman who had given birth to a boy Miriam knew nothing about. To make matters worse, Jake Covington, her adopted son, despised Miriam because she pretended to be a happily married woman. He saw through the hypocrisy of her marriage to Luke.

When Miriam told Beulah that she was going to sell the house and move to Fallon, Nevada, to live with her sister, Marsha, Beulah jumped at the chance to purchase the Covington House, as it was called back then. As soon as Beulah—with Tony's help—purchased the property, Beulah renamed the Covington House as Sarah's Bed and Breakfast.

Beulah and Lloyd had honeymooned in a bed and breakfast in San Diego, California, for two weeks—their wedding gift, compliments of her parents. Beulah never forgot that experience and dreamt of one day having one of her own. That dream of hers became a reality when she opened Sarah's Bed and Breakfast in the summer of 1950.

Years before when Sarah and Ethan lived in their home, before Sarah died, Miriam had brought over their newly adopted son, Jake. He was a quiet boy with a dullard look.

Ethan did not like Jake from the get-go. He did not know at that time just how sick and twisted Jake's mind was.

Ethan had gone into his own bedroom because he did not want to be around Jake. Moments later as he sat on the edge of his bed, Jake came into his bedroom and dropped his trousers and shorts to his knees. He began masturbating in Ethan's face. Ethan jumped to his feet and knocked Jake to his bedroom floor. Ethan never forgot that incident.

Chapter 5

One morning Ethan walked into the Bed and Breakfast through the back door. Beulah had been dusting in the living room. She looked at Ethan and asked, "What's on your mind?"

"I want to make a promise ring for Margo."

Beulah stood thoughtful for a moment. She knew by the tone of Ethan's voice that he was serious about the promise ring. "What birthstones do you want in this promise ring?"

Ethan explained, "I want Mom's birthstone to be on top in the middle, Margo and my birthstones next below, and you and Tony's birthstones next—in that order."

"How much do you want to spend on this promise ring of yours?"

Ethan shrugged his shoulders as he said, "I don't know how much a promise ring costs."

"Neither do I," Beulah said as she opened a telephone book that sat on her desk. She thumbed through the yellow pages until she found a telephone number for Ethel's Fine Jewelry.

"Ethel's Fine Jewelry, how may I help you?" Ethel asked in her baritone voice.

Beulah replied, "I am looking to buy a promise ring having five birthstones in it—for a young man."

After Ethel quoted a price, Beulah thanked her and hung up the receiver.

Beulah looked at Ethan and said, "A promise ring with a gold band and five birthstones is going to cost you anywhere from $50 to $200, depending how fancy of a promise ring you want."

Ethan gasped as he looked at Beulah and said, "I don't have 50 bucks!"

"I do," Beulah said, and quickly added, "Our secret."

The following morning toward the noon hour, Beulah took Ethan to Ethel's Fine Jewelry. As soon as they walked into the jewelry store, Beulah noticed a flyer advertising *Sarah's Bed and Breakfast.* A photograph of Beulah was in the lower left side of the advertisement complete with telephone number to make reservations.

Ethel welcomed Beulah saying, as she gestured to the photograph, "I know folks who have stayed at your place." She paused. "I would love to stay there when Arnold comes home, a second honeymoon."

Beulah removed a business card from her purse and handed it to Ethel. "I'll make room for you and Arnold," she promised.

Ethan had never been to a jeweler before. He was awestruck at the variety of rings with diamonds and other precious stones.

What caught his eye was a display case of high school graduation rings.

"I wonder how much these are," he asked, under his breath. He was so enamored with the rings that he did not notice the small price tags tied to each ring.

Beulah said, "I will get you a class ring when you graduate from high school."

Ethan said to Ethel, "I came here to get a promise ring for Margo, my girlfriend." This was the first time that Ethan mentioned Margo as his girlfriend. He went on to explain to Ethel, "I want five birthstones: Mom's first, then Margo and my birthstones, and Beulah and Tony's birthstones—in that order."

"When are all these birthdays?" Ethel asked Ethan.

"Margo and I have October birthstones."

Beulah said to Ethel, "His mom's birthday was in June. My birthday is in April and Tony's is in March. How long would it take you to fashion this promise ring?"

"How soon do you want the promise ring?" Ethel asked.

"Valentine's Day?" ventured Beulah.

Apologetically Ethel explained, "Morgan, my son, builds my rings. He will not be back until the end of the month."

Ethan was so captivated by all the rings with their precious stones in the display cases that he did not notice Beulah and Ethel talking at the other end of the counter. There were other people in the jewelry store talking to one another in hushed tones, each looking for a special ring to give to a graduating senior, or a wedding or, as in Ethan's case, a promise ring for their girlfriend. *Girls don't give boys promise rings,* Ethan thought. The display cases were well lit, the glass cleaned of all finger prints. A small sign on each of the display cases asked customers not to touch the glass.

Soon Beulah walked over to Ethan and said, "Ethel knew Uncle Luke and Aunt Miriam. This is where Uncle Luke bought all the rings that your aunt wore. After Uncle Luke died, he left your aunt with all the bills and no money to pay them. Miriam had to sell most of the rings to make ends meet."

Ethan looked at Beulah and asked, "How do you know that?"

"Miriam told your mother shortly after Luke died. Later, your mom told me."

Ethan did not want to talk about Luke or Miriam. They were in his past. For a moment, he thought about Jake and then that was all over, too.

Ethel kept an eye on customers as she made her way over to where Ethan and Beulah stood.

Ethan looked at Ethel and asked, "Is this your store?"

Ethel smiled and said, "It is. My grandfather on my mother's side of the family started the business many years ago. When I was old enough, I used to come here after school to be with them until closing time."

Curious, Ethan asked, "Does your husband work here, too?"

"My husband's in the Army. This is his last tour of duty."

Beulah looked at Ethel. "My father was in the Marines."

"Then you know all about military life."

"I certainly do. Where is your husband stationed?" Beulah asked.

"He can't tell me," Ethel said and then added, "I'm ready for him to come home."

"Where did you meet your husband?" Beulah asked.

"Arnold and I have known each other since kindergarten. His parents have a farm just south of here. Five boys and a girl—the youngest. All the boys served in the military. The Army has been good to Arnold, but now he's tired of the many moves we had to make and so am I. My children wanted to come back home to be with their grandparents."

Beulah noted the time on her wristwatch. She looked at Ethel and said, "I need to get back to the Bed and Breakfast. Ethan needs to get back to the restaurant." She paused briefly. "Why don't you and your husband stay at my place after he comes home. I'll make room for you."

"I'll mention it to Arnold in the next letter I write."

Ethan looked at Ethel and asked, "Let me know when the ring is ready, please."

"I certainly will," Ethel said.

On the way back to the Sarah's Bed and Breakfast, Ethan told Beulah, "Don't say anything to Tony about the ring, please."

"I won't."

Chapter 6

A couple arrived one morning while Beulah was checking over the list of scheduled guests. She did a double-take at the woman because for a moment Beulah saw Sarah standing in front of her. The woman's olive-colored skin was soft with no wrinkles and her shoulder-length auburn hair was braided at the back of her head. She wore a white dress with a pattern of forget-me-nots. The man wore a red-checkered flannel shirt under his bib overalls, steel-toed shoes, and used a cane to steady himself.

The woman introduced herself, "I am Nora Pullman." She gestured to the man and said, "This is my husband, Edgar. We found your advertisement in this month's issue of *Sunset* magazine." Nora was thoughtful for a moment before she added, "Edgar encouraged me to come here to see if I was any relation to the Sarah Covington that this Sarah's Bed and Breakfast is named after." She glanced at Edgar for a moment before she added, "Edgar has a diseased heart; the doctors have told us that there is nothing they can do for him."

Nora opened her purse and took out an envelope with the words "Marriage License" written on it. She opened the envelope and removed a piece of paper and handed it to Beulah.

She pointed to her maiden name listed on the marriage license. "You see, my maiden name was Covington." Nora folded her marriage license and put it back into the envelope. Then with reverence she gently placed the envelope back into her purse.

Tony had been cleaning out the hearth and stacking firewood in the black iron basket next to the fireplace when he overheard the conversations between Beulah and the Pullmans.

Tony stood up and introduced himself to Edgar Pullman. "I'm Tony Wong, the handyman around here." He paused as he looked at Nora Pullman and said, "There's a lot of history in this house, but there's also a lot we don't know about Barney Covington and his family. Did you know they were the first settlers in this area?"

Nora explained, "No, I didn't. My mother had a bible with all the names, dates of births, and dates of deaths in it of the Covingtons who were related to her. My father, Edwin Covington, died when I was in my teens. Mom did the best she could to raise us, but she was in poor health, too. I was 18 and my brother was 22 when our mother died. She stated in her will that my brother should have the family bible. He always told me how he would sit down with me when we were youngsters, and we both would read about our grandparents."

"One evening, in the living room of my brother's home, hot embers exploded out over the screen in front of the fireplace and onto the living room carpet, causing it to catch on fire. The family was asleep in their upstairs bedroom. Fortunately, they all got out of the house in time. The bible was destroyed, and the house, too, so I have no reference to my biological family." Nora paused. "That's why we came up here. We thought maybe you would have some knowledge of the information that was lost in the fire."

Sadly, Beulah said, "I'm sorry I can't help you, but I may know someone who can."

Beulah paused. "Let's get you checked in first. This is the slowest time of the year, so you can choose which bedroom you want while you are here."

Tony said to Beulah, "I have to go to the restaurant. I'll take Margo with me. Ethan can help you here. When he is done, have him come to the restaurant."

Beulah gestured to Tony as she smiled at Nora and Edgar Pullman and said, "Margo is Tony's daughter. Ethan and Margo will be down shortly. They are putting the finishing touches on the bedrooms and bathrooms upstairs."

Nora asked Tony, "What kind of restaurant do you have?"

Tony said to Nora, "Peking Duck—we serve a wide range of Chinese food. I have started a new tradition at my restaurant. Every Sunday we now serve a Chinese smorgasbord. Peking Duck is the centerpiece. There is every kind of Asian food at that table, and if there is a favorite Chinese food that is not at the table, I will make it for you."

Edgar said to Tony. "Several times during my naval career my ship visited Hong Kong. That's where I acquired a taste for Chinese food. When I retired, I was transferred to the motor pool at the naval station in San Diego. Nora and I met one evening when I went into the mess hall for dinner."

Beulah said to them, "My father is retired out of the Marine Corps. Several of the ships he was stationed on went to Hong Kong. That was the first time he tasted Chinese food. After he returned home, he took our family out to local Chinese restaurants. Many of them had a smorgasbord of Asian foods."

Edgar looked at Beulah and said, "When I was in Hong Kong, I ate at some of the finest Asian restaurants. Many of them had a smorgasbord type service, too."

Beulah said, "I'll have Ethan take you there for dinner."

"Will you be coming, too?" Nora asked Beulah.

Beulah shook her head and said, "I don't have anyone to cover for me when I'm gone."

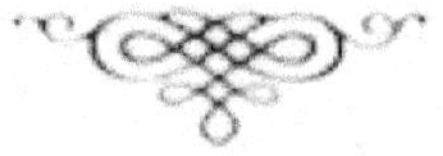

Chapter 7

At that moment, Margo walked into the living room. Beulah introduced her to Nora and Edgar.

"This is Margo, Tony's daughter."

Margo smiled at them and then she looked at Tony and said, "I'm ready, Dad."

Soon, after Tony and Margo left the Bed and Breakfast, Ethan walked into the living room. Beulah introduced him to the Pullmans.

Nora asked Ethan, "Do your parents live around here?"

"My parents died when I was a young boy."

"What happened to them?"

Ethan looked at Nora and said, "My father, Andrew, died of a heart attack one Sunday morning. He went out to the chicken coop to gather eggs for breakfast and that's where it happened. Mom went out to the chicken coop to find out why my father had not returned to the house. She screamed when she saw him lying on the floor of the chicken coop. When I heard her scream, I ran out to the chicken coop. As I stepped inside the coop, she yelled at me to call the sheriff. I ran back into the house and made the telephone call. While I was on the phone, Mom had a seizure and passed out. Her seizure resulted in her having an aneurysm—and that's what eventually killed her."

Nora was taken aback with Ethan's explanation of events. Nora asked, "How did you manage to deal with all that loss at such an early age?"

Ethan hugged Beulah close to him as he looked at Nora and said, "Beulah's the glue that held me together."

Nora said, affectionately, "Edgar has been the glue that held me together. I was a basket case after my parents died. My brother and I have never been close. We're brother and sister, but beyond that we have little in common."

Beulah, not wanting to discuss death and dying, looked at Ethan and suggested, "Why don't you take their luggage upstairs? I told them they could have whatever bedroom they wanted." She looked at Nora and Edgar and said, "When you're ready, we'll talk about family."

Shortly after they left the living room, Officer Carpenter walked into the room. He looked at Beulah and asked, "Is Ethan here?"

Beulah said, "Ethan's upstairs helping our guests get settled in." She paused briefly before asking, "What's this all about?"

"Jake Covington's probation officer called my office yesterday afternoon. Jake wants to make amends with Ethan."

Beulah gave Officer Carpenter a wayward glance as she asked, "Jake's returning to Covington?"

"His probation officer told me that Jake is a changed man."

Beulah walked over to the stairs that led up to the bedrooms upstairs and called Ethan to come down to the living room.

When Ethan walked into the living room, Officer Carpenter said to him, "Jake wants to come back home. His probation officer told me Jake is a changed man."

Ethan looked at Officer Carpenter. "He can talk to me anytime he wants. I'm a black belt now."

Beulah looked at Ethan and said, "Tony needs you at the restaurant. But before you go, would you build a fire in the fireplace, please?"

Ethan crumpled newspapers inside the fireplace and placed fire starters over the newspaper and then the dried wood from the wrought iron basket. He removed a box of matches from the hearth above the fireplace. He stuck a match on the side of the match box and put the flame to the newspaper. Shortly, there was a roaring fire in the fireplace hearth.

"Thank you," Beulah called out after Ethan as he walked out of the living room.

After Ethan had gone, Officer Carpenter asked Beulah, "How's business?"

Beulah said, "In the beginning it was slow, but this past holiday season most of our rooms were taken. Gary and Heather Souls have given me a lot of advertisement in the *Covington Banner* in exchange for a room here." She paused and then offered, "Why don't you bring your wife and spend a weekend with us?"

Officer Carpenter said, "I'll take you up on that invitation. My wife and I have never had a proper honeymoon."

Beulah asked, "What's your wife's first name?"

Office Carpenter said, "Claire, her first name is Claire. We were married on Valentine's Day, Tuesday, February 14, 1922."

"Where did you meet Claire?" Beulah asked.

"Claire was the dispatcher in the police department when we met. She's two years older than me. On our anniversaries, we go to Tony's restaurant."

"Celebrate your honeymoon here," Beulah offered.

Officer Carpenter said, "I'll mention your offer to Claire, and see what she says. I'm sure she would be delighted to stay here. I'll get back to you soon."

"I want to show you something before you go," Beulah said as she walked over to the fireplace mantel. "I found this metal box in the old garage just before it was torn down." She stepped to one side so Officer Carpenter could look over the contents of the box.

"Was there anything else in the box?"

Beulah shrugged and said, "Just these things."

"You have a good mystery going on here. I'm sure you'll discover a family secret or two." Officer Carpenter glanced at his wristwatch. "It's time for me to get back on patrol."

While Nora and Edgar were upstairs unpacking their clothes, Beulah phoned Gary Souls to brief him about Nora and Edgar Pullman.

A brief time later Gary and his wife, Heather, arrived at the Sarah's Bed and Breakfast. Heather carried a backpack and a camera that was attached to the backpack.

Beulah made them comfortable in the living room in front of the fireplace. Beulah walked over to the fireplace mantel. She brought the metal box back with her. She sat down on the davenport between Gary and Heather and said, "I found this box in the old garage."

She removed the lid as she handed the box to them and said, "I would like to find out who Rose C. was."

After Heather and Gary examined the contents of the box, Heather looked at Beulah and said, "I love a good mystery."

Gary said to Beulah, "Heather has read all of Agatha Christie's books."

Heather looked at Gary and said, excitedly, "Let's find out who Rose C. was."

"Okay! We can do this," Gary said to Heather.

Just then the Pullmans came back into the living room. Gary and Heather stood as Beulah introduced them.

Gary explained to Nora and Edgar that there were very few records of Barney Covington and his family after he arrived here. Gary suggested that Nora should visit Elsa Meyers, the school librarian and chairperson of the Covington Historical Society. If anyone could shed some light on this matter, she'd be the one.

Chapter 8

Elsa Meyers was the third generation of Meyers to live in the town of Covington. Elsa's great grandparents were early settlers. They came to the area in a covered wagon. They became close friends with Barney Covington, who was the first white settler in the area. However, Elsa's great grandparents never wrote down what the area was like or anything concerning Barney Covington, his wife, or his five sons—Barney, Jr., Andrew, Luke, Edwin, and Joseph.

Elsa Meyers established the Covington Historical Society. Her historical society met in the living room of her home. After just a few sessions, the Society fell apart because the members became increasing frustrated with the lack of records of the Covington families. Some members of the Society had their own agendas and wanted to talk about their own families. When Elsa urged them to focus on the Covingtons, the Society members—except for Elsa—gave up on the Historical Society.

Gary telephoned Elsa and asked if he and the Pullmans could come over to her home and talk to her about her Historical Society. They were interested in examining whatever documents she might have concerning the Covington families.

Elsa regretfully admitted to Gary that she had few documents of the Covington families, but they were welcome to come over anyway.

The following afternoon Gary, Heather, Edgar, and Nora sat in the living room of Elsa's home. Elsa showed Nora and Edgar the few historical references she had found about Barney Covington.

Elsa noticed a discolored piece of yellow paper that she had previously overlooked. Penciled on the yellowed paper was a reference to a *Ruth Covington*, but there was no indication of who Ruth Covington was or where she lived—if, in fact, she was still alive.

After looking over the few references that Elsa produced, Gary thanked Elsa for her time. When they returned to Sarah's Bed and Breakfast, Gary offered to help the Pullmans locate this Ruth woman.

The following day, after a thorough examination of court records at the county archives—going back to the Spanish American War—Gary and Heather came across a marriage license issued to Trevor Martin Souls and Ruth Anne Covington. Gary wondered if Trevor was his great grandfather and if so, how come he had never heard of Trevor before.

Acting on a hunch, Gary thumbed through the telephone directory where he found an address for Twilight Retirement Home, the only nursing home in Covington, run by a local charity. Gary telephoned the retirement home to ask if there was a Ruth Anne Covington Souls living there.

After Gary waited for several moments, the director of the Twilight Retirement Home came on the phone and confirmed to him that Ruth Anne Covington Souls was one of their residents, but that she was in failing health. She added that no living relatives were listed among Ruth's emergency contacts.

In an air of excitement Gary, Heather, and the Pullmans arranged with the Twilight Retirement Home director to visit Ruth Covington the next day. The home was staffed with nursing caretakers and was on the same property as the hospital.

As they entered the lobby of the Twilight Retirement Home, they approached the Information Desk.

Gary looked at the nurse who sat at the desk and said, "We understand that you have a Ruth Covington Souls living here as one of your residents." Gary gestured to Nora and Edgar Pullman and added, "We believe these folks are relatives of hers."

The nurse thumbed through the Rolodex. When she located the room where Ruth was located, she looked at Gary said, "I'll take you to her room."

Ruth sat in a wheelchair with a crocheted afghan of red, blue, and white stripes that covered her legs. There were many photographs hanging on the wall of her room. Ruth wheeled her chair closer to the wall. Pointing to each one, Ruth gave a brief explanation of the pictures of relations now long since gone. There was one photograph taken of her husband, Trevor Martin Souls.

"Oh, my gosh!" Gary said as he pointed to one of the photographs of a man standing beside a printing press.

"That's my uncle, dad's brother, Leroy."

"You never met him?" Ruth asked.

"The Souls were a large family. But for some reason they were never a close-knit bunch. When Heather and I began dating, I told her that I had one condition to our marriage, I wanted us to be best friends first and then lovers."

Ruth said, "Trevor was my soul mate. He was the editor and sole proprietor of his newspaper called *The Voice*. His newspaper had human interest stories about the people in the area and was paid for by local business owners." Ruth went on to explain that Trevor's newspaper met with some local resistance from those in the community, especially some of the Covingtons, who thought the content of the newspaper was too folksy. When he refused to print what the Covingtons and other businesses wanted to be printed, they withdrew their financial support of *The Voice,* and the newspaper died.

Ruth was always Trevor's rock when things went wrong, but when *The Voice* died, Trevor died, too. Ruth gave Gary the last copy of *The Voice* she had, along with some other news clippings that never found their way into the newspaper.

The following day Gary wrote an article on the front page of the *Covington Banner* in which he described Ruth and Trevor Martin Souls and *The Voice*. Over time, Gary would do reprints from *The Voice* that gave an account of what was important in the town of Covington on any given day.

Beulah was particularly fascinated by this newly uncovered local history about the town of Covington and its residents—so much so, that she decided to go to Gary with a proposition.

Gary, with Heather's help, created a colorful brochure of the Bed and Breakfast. When they showed a draft of the brochure to Beulah, she was thoughtful for a moment because there was something missing in the photograph that should be there, but what, she could not remember. She thanked Gary and Heather for taking the time to show her the draft of the brochure.

When Beulah offered to pay Gary for the cost of the brochure he told her, "It's good advertisement for the newspaper and for you, too. We're all in this together, so let's make it work for both of our businesses."

Heather mailed a copy of the brochure to *Sunset Magazine* to see if they would be interested in publishing the brochure's information. Months later the brochure itself would appear in *Sunset Magazine*. Beulah began to receive even more reservations from readers of *Sunset Magazine*.

In the meantime, Heather placed copies of the brochure in downtown businesses where she got the owner's permission.

One of those locations was Ethel's Fine Jewelry, the place where Gary purchased the engagement ring and later the wedding ring that he had given to Heather on the day they were married.

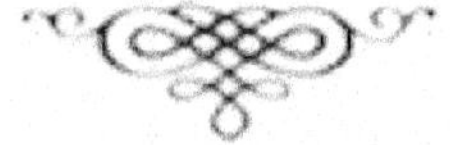

Chapter 9

A groundskeeper and his wife lived in a small home across the street from the Graceland Park Cemetery. They were there every day except on Sundays to keep the cemetery plots clean and the area between the plots weeded and mowed.

A small building stood in the middle of the cemetery. On a desk inside the building were ledgers that marked all the graves and who were buried there. On shelves nearby, there were cards and fresh flowers and vases to hold the flowers. Vases were placed in holes next to each grave. When the flowers died, the groundskeeper removed them.

Beulah had come to the Graceland Park Cemetery to get away from the bed and breakfast for a while, to come sit, to think, and to talk to the person she missed and loved.

It was a sunny day, just above freezing, and no wind. Beulah wore layers of clothing, a hooded coat, wool gloves, and galoshes over her shoes. A wide-brimmed hat shielded her eyes from the sun's glare. The frozen ground was covered with several inches of old snow that crunched under her feet as she walked along. When she arrived at the graveside where Sarah and Andrew lay, she sat down on a wooden bench that Tony had placed there shortly after Sarah was laid to rest. With her gloved hands, Beulah brushed the snow off the top of the grave markers.

Beulah soliloquized, *"Ethan graduates at the end of this school year. I know you and Andrew will be with him in his graduation cap and gown as he receives his high school diploma. Margo and Ethan will be married after he graduates. I want to hold their wedding reception at Sarah's Bed and Breakfast."* Beulah struggled with her thoughts as she said, *"Tony had a stoke awhile back. The doctor told me later that Tony has heart disease."* Beulah rested her forehead against the grave marker as she looked down at the flowers she had placed there. She cried out aloud, *"I don't want to be here when Tony dies."*

Beulah had no idea how prophetic her words just spoken were.

"I found a metal box in the old garage that had Rose C. written on its cover. You wouldn't happen to know who she was, would you? Sometimes, when I'm all alone, I hear your voice from the other side talking to me about whatever is on your mind, like we used to do. I met some new people, Edgar and Nora Pullman. She showed me her marriage license that said she was a Covington before she married Edgar. She reminds me so much of you. Jake is back in our lives. I wish there was some way to get rid of him forever."

Beulah removed a handkerchief from her coat pocket to wipe her tears away and blow her nose. She remained at the gravesite for a while longer then finally she stood up and kissed Sarah's name and returned to the bed and breakfast.

Chapter 10

Gary invested his own money into printing a coffee table book about Sarah's Bed and Breakfast and the town of Covington. He had also moved all the records of Elsa's Historical Society into the *Covington Banner* so that she could have her own office there.

Gary gave Beulah a copy of the publication to place on the coffee table in the living room of Sarah's Bed and Breakfast. He also set up a book exhibit in the Bed and Breakfast (with Beulah's permission) for guests to purchase a copy of the book at the front desk when they arrived.

After Heather took a copy to the library, the librarian called the next day asking for more copies because people wanted to read about their town's history.

Several days later a young man brought an elderly woman into Gary's office. He wore coveralls, a blue-checkered flannel shirt and shoes that had a dull luster to them. The woman was clothed in a full-length floral printed dress, her brightly rouged cheeks and blue eyes were full of life. She wore her full-length auburn hair in a braid that rested against her back.

The young man handed Gary a worn accordion folder that was full of papers. He looked at Gary and introduced himself, "I am Peter Souls, Leroy's son, and this is my grandmother, Myrtle-Marie. I always wanted to know what you were like."

Myrtle-Marie smiled at Gary and said, "Please don't call me Myrtle. I was given the name of two of my grandmothers who hated one another."

"Why did they hate each another?" Gary asked as he offered his chair to Myrtle-Marie.

"Myrtle came from a devout Catholic family. Marie's family were Pentecostal people who believed the pope was the anti-Christ." She paused. "I'm not here to talk about them. I want to talk to you about Barney Covington." She sat down on Gary's chair. There were several other chairs in the office. Heather, with her writing pad in hand, sat down next to Gary.

Myrtle-Marie rested the accordion folder on her lap. Her hands shook as she opened the folder.

"Let me help," Gary offered.

"The older I get, the more I shake but my memory," she tapped the side of her head with her finger, "is as sharp as ever!"

"What is here that would be of interest to me?" Gary asked.

Gary sat stunned while Heather's jaw dropped open when Myrtle-Marie looked at Gary and said, "I am the daughter of one of Barney Covington's sons. Barney was a career Army officer. He was a Pentecostal minister, too. He believed the Constitution of the United States was as sacred as the Bible. He believed Abraham Lincoln was preordained and predestined by God to save the Union. He retired out of the Union Army one week after President Lincoln was assassinated. His wife had died of dysentery the month before. She worked in an Army infirmary as a nurse and contacted the disease while treating solders."

"He named his home Covington House. That house became a meeting house for farmers to gather and talk about what they wanted for themselves and their families. Six months later the farmers elected Barney Covington as the first mayor of Covington. They elected a town council, a postmaster, sheriff, and then they built a bank that was known as the Farmers Mercantile bank. Barney along with a group of other men traveled to the state capital. They petitioned the state for a charter of Covington County with the county seat in the town of Covington. Barney was sworn in as a state representative from Covington County."

"It is all here," she said, gesturing to the papers Gary held in his lap. "My throat is dry."

Heather brought a glass of water to Myrtle-Marie.

"Thank you," she said as she sipped the water. While Gary thumbed through the papers, Myrtle-Marie looked at Gary and said, "I have a sister, but I don't know where she lives."

"Who might that be?" Gary asked.

"Ruth Covington. She's my sister."

Gary and Heather glanced at each other. They both started to talk when Heather looked at Gary and said, "Go ahead."

"Heather and I met Ruth. She was a Covington before she married Trevor Martin Souls, my grandfather. Trevor started a newspaper called . . ."

"*The Voice*," Myrtle-Marie interrupted. 'I know all about that *little* newspaper. Did Ruth tell you why the newspaper died?"

Gary said, "Lack of financial support."

"From the Covingtons?" Myrtle-Marie asked.

"That's what Ruth told us," Heather said.

"Ruth and I were always jealous of one another," pausing briefly as she cleared her throat. Gary handed the glass of water to Myrtle-Marie who took a swig and handed the glass back to Gary. She continued. "The rift between Ruth and me happened over a Thanksgiving dinner. Ruth always cooked the Thanksgiving dinner. One Thanksgiving I asked Ruth if I could prepare the holiday dinner. The following Thanksgiving, I prepared the dinner in my home. The dinner was far better than hers, but she never admitted that to family or friends. Ruth and I have never spoken to one another since then."

Gary looked at Peter and asked, "Did you know about this?"

Peter gently squeezed his grandmother's hand as he looked at Gary and said, "Grandma told me the story when she thought I was old enough to understand. I think grandma should find her sister. It's a wound that needs to be healed."

As Gary placed all the paperwork back into the accordion folder, Myrtle-Marie said, "You can keep those papers and perhaps someday you'll want to tell your readers about how the newspaper died."

The following morning Gary and Heather sat in Ruth's room. After a few awkward moments, Gary looked at Ruth and said, "I had a visit from Myrtle-Marie yesterday in my office."

Ruth said, "My sister and I are old women who need to put the past behind us."

"Who's older?" Heather asked, notebook and pencil in hand.

"She's a year older than me." Ruth moved her wheelchair over to the wall where the family photographs hung. She pointed to a photograph that neither Gary nor Heather had noticed before. "That is the only photograph I have of my sister and me. The man between us is Trevor." She looked at Gary and said, "Yes, I want to see my sister."

The following afternoon Gary and Heather brought Myrtle-Marie and Peter to the nursing home. Ruth knew nothing about Peter. Over time the two sisters had put aside their differences.

Myrtle-Marie told Gary later that she needed to find a place to live. Peter had been taking care of her, but that was becoming unfair to him. He was always at his grandmother's side. He was a senior in high school and always wanted to be a police officer but had no idea how to achieve that goal. Later Gary would introduce Peter to Officer Carpenter. Eventually, Officer Carpenter nominated Peter to the police academy.

Heather used her influence to place Myrtle-Marie in the Twilight Nursing Home. The director of the nursing home moved the two sisters into a larger residence so they could be together.

Over the next several weeks Gary wrote a series of articles that appeared on the front page of the *Covington Banner* about how love and forgiveness brought two sisters together.

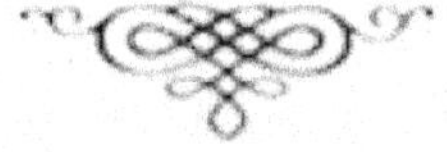

Chapter 11

One afternoon after Beulah and Ethan returned to the Bed and Breakfast from running errands, a couple came in. The middle-aged man wore a military uniform that had several rows of ribbons on it. Beulah recognized three of the ribbons as the Navy cross, silver star and purple heart. A caduceus on his rating told Beulah he was a hospital corpsman with combat experience.

Beulah looked at the man and said, "Welcome to Sarah's Bed and Breakfast." After she had them sign the register, she glanced at their names that read Mr. and Mrs. Bud and Irene Silverman. Beulah looked at Ethan as she gestured to Bud Silverman and said, "He's a Navy guy and those six gold stripes on his sleeve tell me that he has over twenty-four years in service."

"You a Navy gal?" Bud asked Beulah.

Beulah smiled and said, "My late husband was a Navy pilot and my father is a retired Marine. My father had profound respect for Navy hospital corpsman. He often told me that there were two people in any unit that the enemy wanted killed. One was the radio operator and the other was the hospital corpsman."

Bud looked at Beulah and said, "I was assigned to the Marine barracks the morning of December 7, 1942, when the Japanese bombed Pearl Harbor. My closest friend was with me. During the attack, he was killed when a piece of shrapnel that had been torn off from one of the firetrucks sliced him in half. To this day I remember that incident as if it were yesterday." Bud fought back tears and Irene held him close to her side.

Beulah threw her hand to her face as tears welled up in her eyes as she said, "I am so sorry."

Irene said, "Some days are easier that others but we manage to get through them all." Pausing she looked at Bud and added, "Don't we?" and kissed his forehead.

Ethan stood in awe in that moment. He had no way of knowing that Bud Silverman was going to change his life forever.

Beulah invited them to sit in the breakfast nook. Ethan made a pot of coffee and then brought over a bamboo tray with blueberry muffins. Once the coffee was made, Ethan filled four cups and took them, two cups at a time, to the breakfast nook. He brought a creamer from the refrigerator and sugar to the table.

Beulah sat across from them and asked, "How long are you looking to stay? We have rooms available, if you would like to stay here."

Bud glanced at Irene and then said to Beulah, "My retirement orders sent me here to manage the Navy recruiting station."

Ethan looked at Bud and said, "I didn't know we had a recruiting station in town."

Beulah explained to Ethan, "The new shopping mall has a unit for all of the branches of the service." She stood up and walked over to the counter that the register was on. As she handed Bud the *Covington Banner* she said, "Homes for sale are listed in the newspaper. After you and Irene have settled in, I'll have Gary and Heather Souls come over."

Beulah paused as she looked at Ethan and said, "Ethel called. Your promise ring is ready."

"Who's your girlfriend?" Bud asked Ethan.

Ethan blushed as he said, "Margo Wong."

"Do we get to meet her?" Irene asked.

"Someday." Ethan said and then asked Beulah, "Can we go get the ring?"

After they got the Silvermans settled in their room, Beulah took Ethan to the jewelry store. Ethan stood reverently at the counter in Ethel's jewelers as he held the ring in the palms of his hands. Ethel smiled at how pleased Ethan was with the ring.

Once outside the jewelry store, Ethan looked at Beulah and said excitedly, "I want to give the ring to Margo now."

Beulah mused, “Why don’t you wait awhile until the time is right.”

“When will that be?” Ethan asked.

Beulah hugged Ethan close to her. Her eyes watered when she said, “You’ll know.”

When Ethan returned to the Peking Duck, he found Margo sitting at one of the tables, working a crossword puzzle. Ethan did his best to have a poker face as he sat done next to Margo. The promise ring was in his pants pocket.

“How is your day?” Margo asked as she continued to work the crossword puzzle.

Ethan said, “I’ve been with Beulah.”

“What are you hiding from me?” Margo asked.

Ethan playfully shrugged as he said, “Nothing.”

Margo scrunched her face as she looked at Ethan and said, “You’re no good at keeping secrets from me.”

Ethan had been in love with Margo the first day he met her.

Chapter 12

The morning after Beulah took Ethan to the Ethel's Fine Jewelry to pick up the promise ring, Bud asked Beulah, "How well do you know Gary and Heather Souls?"

Beulah explained, "They're publishers of the *Covington Banner,* our local newspaper, a nice couple."

Irene and Bud sat at the breakfast nook drinking coffee and eating one of Beulah's blackberry-walnut muffins that she had baked earlier that morning.

Their cups of coffee and muffins sat on top of the *Covington Banner* in the *Homes for Sale* section. Irene circled several homes in pencil that she and Bud were interested in and wanted to look at. After they finished their breakfast, Irene folded the newspaper and placed it in her purse.

As they stood up to leave, Irene looked at Beulah and said, "You have a wonderful place here. I don't know how long we'll be gone."

"I'll see you when you return. If I'm in bed, just make yourselves at home."

Bud looked at Beulah and asked, "Why don't you have a television?"

"It's a distraction," Beulah began. "I want people to get to know one another, become friends and leave here with good memories. You can't do that while you're watching television."

Irene said. "I agree that here a television is a distraction. We have one in our home that we watch in the evening around the fireplace."

Beulah asked, "What are your favorite programs?"

Irene boasted, "We like sports channels. When I was in high school, I was on the swim and track teams," Irene boasted playfully. "I won first place from freshman through my senior year."

Bud said, "I excelled in swimming, too. Played a lot of football and baseball." He hugged Irene close to him and said, "just an average guy…"

Irene held Bud close to her. "You're my average guy and my soul mate, too." They kissed and she added, "We need to get going."

Bud was quiet for the first part of the day. He seemed to be deep in thought and anxious at times, too. At first Irene became anxious, too. She kept her thoughts to herself until she couldn't stand Bud's quietness. Finally, she looked at Bud and asked, "What is wrong with you?"

Bud may appear to be the pillar of strength to people who did not know him but deep down inside he as a loving, caring man, even to other men.

Bud suggested, "Let's have lunch at the Peking Duck." That was fine with Irene—anything to get Bud to calm down and talk about whatever it was that was bothering him.

Once at the Peking Duck, Bud and Irene sat at a small round table. Bud leaned back in his wooden chair, closed his eyes for a moment. When he opened his eyes, he removed his wallet from his denim trousers back pocket and opened it on the table. He removed a business card that read, "Sarah's Bed and Breakfast, *Beulah Anderson,* Proprietor." Tears welled up in his eyes as he said to Irene, "I want to know who her father is."

Irene asked, "Why?"

"As I lay there on the tarmac, everything was spinning around me and then I passed out. Hours later as I lay in the infirmary, a Marine medic tended to my wounds. A nurse later told me that I would have died if it had not been for this medic. When I asked the nurse the name of the medic, she brought him over to me. His name tag read, *Julius Anderson.* I wonder if that man was Beulah's father."

"Let's go back and then you can ask Beulah if this man was her father."

"I wonder if he is still alive," Bud paused and said, "Let's go house shopping before we return to the bed and breakfast."

It was late in the afternoon when Bud and Irene returned to the bed and breakfast. They sat at the breakfast nook. Bud brought two glasses of chilly water to the nook. Soon Beulah walked into the kitchen.

"I don't sleep sound because my mind never shuts down. I'm always thinking about what needs to be done around here." Beulah threw her hands in the air as she said, "You don't need to listen to my problems," she paused and then asked excitedly, "Did you find a home?"

Irene looked at Beulah, smiled and said, "We did! It has three bedrooms, a spacious kitchen with plenty of counter space with a refrigerator and freezer, clothes washer and dryer, and even a dishwasher. When I was growing up on our farm, we never had any of those appliances. We had an icebox. Mom had a water pump in the utility room next to the kitchen where she drew water from our well into a large kettle that she put on the kitchen stove to heat water. Oh," she said fondly. "I had a happy childhood filled with *good* memories."

Bud asked Beulah, "Was your father's name Julius Anderson?" followed by, "Is he still alive?"

Beulah replied, "It is, and yes, he is still alive. Why do you ask?"

"He saved my life the morning the Japanese bombed Pearl Harbor."

Beulah picked up the telephone that sat on top of the register. She dialed her parents' telephone number. After several rings, she heard her father's voice on the other end.

She said, "Dad, I have a gentleman here who says he remembers you from that awful morning the Japanese bombed Pearl Harbor."

"What's his name?"

"Bud Silverman. His name is Bud Silverman."

Beulah heard her father begin to cry while he said, "Put him on the phone."

Bud's hands shook as he put the receiver to his ear and said in a shaky voice, "Julius? Is this really you?"

"It is," Julius said. In his mind's eye, he recalled that moment as though it was yesterday.

"We need to get together," Bud said. He paused for a moment and then added, "I don't sleep much at night, things stress me out like shopping for a home, or being out in public. I'm not the social one," he tenderly touched Irene's hand as he said, "Irene is."

Julius said, "I don't sleep much at night either. There are some nights I cry myself to sleep."

Softly Bud spoke as tears welled up in his eyes, "I go through the same nights, too."

Julius said, "Let me talk to my daughter, please."

Beulah listened as Julius said, "Mom and I haven't had a vacation in a long time. "Would you mind if we come up this summer for a couple of weeks?"

Beulah cuffed the receiver as she looked at Bud and Irene and whispered, "Mom and Dad want to come up this summer."

Bud motioned for the receiver from Beulah.

"Irene and I just bought a home. Come stay with us. I make the best BBQ beef ribs. Irene makes the best BBQ beans I've ever tasted. How about we all get together this coming Fourth of July in our new home? Does Tami make coleslaw?"

"She does," Julius replied, and then Julius asked, "Does Beulah have a boyfriend?"

"She does," Bud said and handed the receiver to her.

Beulah said, "His name is Tony Wong. He's my best friend and my lover," she paused as she heard the back-door open. She knew who those footsteps belonged to.

Tony sat down next to her. Tears welled up in her eyes as she said, "He's with me now, Dad."

"Put him on the phone."

"That's a Chinese name, isn't it?"

"It is," Tony replied and then asked, "How much do you want to know about me?"

"What do you do for a living?"

"I own a Chinese restaurant here in Covington. I serve Cantonese, Mandarin, and Szechuan food. My specialty is Peking Duck. Do you like Chinese food?" Tony asked.

"I do. We have a large variety of Chinese cuisine in San Diego. Tami's favorite is Mandarin and egg drop soup. How long have you been dating Beulah?"

"We're not dating, just close friends. I have a daughter, Margo, who's been working at the restaurant since she was old enough to wash dishes. She, along with Ethan, Sarah's son, do all the prep cooking and serve food. I have a dedicated staff who have been with me long enough to know the routine. Turnover is rare." He paused. "Before you ask, Beulah should talk to you about her friend, Sarah."

As Tony handed the receiver to Beulah he covered the receiver with the palm of his hand and said, "My bowels are talking to me."

Beulah explained to Julius, "I met Sarah Covington shortly after I arrived in Covington. Andrew, her husband, had a heart attack on a Sunday morning while he was out in the chicken coop, gathering eggs. Luke and Miriam Covington took Sarah into a home that Luke owned." Beulah broke down and cried into the telephone receiver. "I can't talk about this anymore."

Julius choked back his tears, too, as he said, "Let's wait until your mom and I come up. What does your summer look like?"

Beulah wiped her face with a napkin and then said, "I'll make room for you and Mom."

"I'm retired now, so my time is my own. Let me talk to Bud again. We'll talk more, very soon."

After Beulah excused herself from the breakfast nook, Julius, Bud and Tony talked on the telephone for the rest of the afternoon. Beulah never asked what the three men talked about.

Beulah had been unable to sleep after Bud and Irene had gone to bed. She leaned back in the breakfast nook bench and gazed out the window. A flood light illuminated the front yard. The lawn was covered in old snow, a light breeze blew what snow that was on left on tree branches to the ground and in that moment two deer, a doe and a fawn, came into the front yard.

Beulah was so mesmerized that she did not hear Irene tiptoe into the kitchen. Irene pressed a finger to her lips as she walked up to the breakfast nook. The two of them watched in wonderment as the doe and the fawn pranced out of the yard.

Beulah said, "They've been here before, maybe not those same two."

Irene looked at Beulah and said, "I love Bud, but there are times when I need a woman friend to talk to things over." Beulah patted the bench with the palm of her hand as she said, "I'm a good listener."

After Irene sat next to Beulah she said, "I want a new life for Bud once he retires. There must be something for him to do here."

The answer to Irene's question would come the following morning when Gary and Heather Souls came to the Bed and Breakfast. Gary was constantly looking for a human-interest story, something that would appeal to his readers. Beulah had cleared off the breakfast nook table. Gary and Heather sat one side, Bud and Irene on the opposite side. Beulah had made coffee and baked apple-walnut muffins earlier in the morning. Gary and Heather knew the lay of the kitchen.

Beulah needed to go into town for groceries. She thought it best that the Souls and Silvermans should be alone. Initially Gary thought that the interview would only take an hour or so but after just an hour, Gary realized he had a landmark story to tell his readers. Over the next few days Gary and Heather would return and in time, Gary and Heather would become close friends to Bud and Irene Silverman.

In the first installment of the *Covington Banner,* the headlines read: WWII hero comes to our community. There were several installments about Bud Silverman's military life. In the first article that Gary wrote, he noted that Bud Silverman had been born and raised in a small farming community not far from the town of Covington. Bud did not want to be a farmer, not that he did not respect farmers, he just did not want to be one of them. He wanted to travel and see what was in the rest of the world. He always wanted to know what was over the next hill. He met Irene while he was on active duty shortly after he had graduated out of basic training in San Diego, California. She was a nurse at the base hospital where she first met Bud, and in that instant, they fell in love.

By the time that the third article appeared in the *Covington Banner* about Bud Silverman, Gary was flooded with hundreds of letters from his readers who agreed that Bud Silverman should go into politics.

On a hunch, Gary invited Irene and Bud to the *Covington Banner* to discuss Bud's future in Covington.

"What do you see as a future for you and Irene here?" Gary asked.

Bud knew a leading question when he heard one.

"What do you have in mind?" Bud asked.

Gary said, "I want you to run for mayor."

Irene's face glowed, her voice was full of excitement as she said to Bud, "You would make a good mayor. You're a decent and honest man and you are one of these folks—you were born and raised on a farm not too far from here—you're a veteran who holds the nation's second highest award, the silver star, and several purple hearts."

"A shoo-in," Heather said.

Gary stood up and walked over to a liquor cabinet and removed four etched glasses monogrammed with printing presses on them and a bottle of Lagavulin, a 16-year old single-malt scotch whiskey. He poured a jigger of scotch into each glass and handed a glass to everyone.

Gary gestured to Bud, saying, "The best is yet to come."

Bud looked at Gary and said, "I can't run for political office until I retire."

Gary answered, "I know that, but when the time comes, would you consider running for mayor?"

Bud touched Gary's scotch glass with his as he said, "It's a deal."

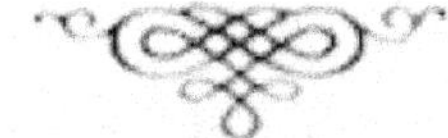

Chapter 13

On Valentine's Day, Officer Carpenter and his wife, Claire, arrived at the Bed and Breakfast in the early afternoon. After they settled in, they came back down to the living room. They stood by the fireplace and warmed their hands by the fire.

The Carpenters were tall people. Officer Carpenter's cheeks had a ruddy tone with a boyish look. Claire wore a hint of makeup and her hair was in a French braid. They both wore casual attire.

"Everyone settled in?" Beulah asked as she walked into the living room. She carried a bamboo tray with carrot-walnut muffins and coffee. As she set the tray down on the coffee table, she looked up at them and asked, "Do either of you take cream or sugar?"

Officer Carpenter smiled at Beulah and said, "We like our coffee black."

Claire looked at Beulah and said, "I finally get to meet the woman my husband talks about." She paused briefly and then asked, "Will you join us for dinner this evening?"

"I will," Beulah replied. "Ethan is going to stay here and watch over the place while I'm celebrating your wedding anniversary." Beulah looked at Officer Carpenter and said, "I've always known you as Officer Carpenter. What is your first name? You don't mind me asking, do you?"

Officer Carpenter said in a matter-of-fact tone of voice, "It's Samantha. My parents were certain they were going to have a girl, so they never thought of a boy's name. My family and close friends call me Sam." Officer Carpenter smiled at Beulah as he said, "You can call me Sam."

They were interrupted when Ethan came in through the back door.

"Hi, Ethan."

Officer Carpenter looked at Beulah and asked, "How did you know it was Ethan?"

Ethan laughed as he looked at Officer Carpenter and said, "Beulah knows my walk."

When he noticed the tray with carrot-walnut muffins and coffee, he glanced over to Beulah, who said, "Help yourself."

Officer Carpenter looked at Ethan and asked, "What are you going to do after you graduate from high school?"

Ethan sat down on a rocking chair next to an end table. He took a sip of his coffee and a bite out of his muffin, looked at Officer Carpenter and said, "Keep doing what I'm doing now. After I graduate, Margo and I want to get married and start a family of our own." He paused as he looked at Beulah and said,

"Margo and I want to move into my mom's home after we're married."

"Do you two have a wedding date?" Beulah asked.

"Sometime after I graduate this spring."

They were interrupted when Bud and Irene walked into the living room. Irene boasted as she patted Bud on his back, "Our future Mayor. Gary Souls wants Bud to run for mayor after he's retired!"

Beulah walked up to Bud and gave him a hug and as she did this, Bud looked at her and said, "I will never forget the hospitality you have given to Irene and me."

Beulah answered, "You are part of an extended family. We're all different in our own ways but still the same."

Ethan wanted to talk with Bud about a career in the Navy. That conversation would come later when Ethan had the opportunity to sit down with Bud.

Later that day Beulah, the Carpenters, and the Silvermans left for the evening for the restaurant to celebrate Sam and Claire's wedding anniversary.

After they all left, Ethan walked around the Bed and Breakfast. He knew every nook and cranny in the building. Soon he walked into the kitchen and started making an avocado dip when a knock on the front door caught his attention. He set the dip and potato chips on the coffee table in front of the davenport and walked towards the front door.

Ethan's heart skipped a beat when he opened the door and in front of him stood Jake Covington. Jake was a tall thin man, thinner than when Ethan saw him last. He was clean shaven and there was a sparkle in his eyes. His thick red hair was permed. He wore a hint of musk cologne, which was Ethan's cologne of choice, too.

They stood there staring at each other for a few seconds when Jake said, "I know it's late, but I wanted to stop by."

Ethan's mind was spinning wildly. He remembered the time when Jake tried to kill him. But that incident happened years before and now Ethan, a black belt, knew how to defend himself. It was a stiff conversation between them because Ethan knew that Jake was not there *just* for a visit.

Jake gave the room a once-over and that is when he caught sight of the metal box sitting on the fireplace mantle. He stood up and walked towards the fireplace mantle.

"What's this?" he asked as he opened the metal box.

"Beulah found that box in the old garage." Ethan noticed Jake's stiff stance, the hair on the back of Jake's neck bristled.

"You okay?" Ethan asked.

Jake turned to face Ethan and said, smiling, "I'm fine." He lied. He was full of rage, hatred.

Meanwhile, the Carpenters celebrated their wedding anniversary at the Peking Duck. Beulah waited and bused tables along with other employees that Tony had trained when he needed extra help. They were students at the local junior college who were enrolled in the culinary arts program.

Kenneth Richardson, the culinary arts instructor, was a close friend of Tony's because of his love of Chinese food. The students got extra credit in Richardson's culinary arts program if they accepted Richardson's offer of hands-on experience by working at one of the town's many restaurants. None of the work-study students had ever eaten Chinese food because most of them were raised on meat and potatoes with some other vegetables. This semester Kenneth Richardson had his students put together a cookbook that would showcase recipes from family and friends. There would be a section on Chinese cuisine. After the cookbook was published, Kenneth Richardson placed the cookbooks throughout bookstores in town. The cookbooks sold at a reasonable price that anyone who wanted one could afford.

It was late in the evening. One of the culinary students turned the *Open* sign to *Closed* and started to pull down window shades. Beulah instructed the students to clean all the tables. Claire and Beulah sat down at a small rectangular table across the room from where Officer Carpenter and Bud Silverman sat.

Beulah asked Claire, "How long has . . ." she could not bring herself to say "Sam."

Claire, being gracious about the issue, said, "As soon as he graduated out of high school he applied to the police academy.

His father is a retired chief of police. Sam never used his father as a reference. He wanted to be accepted into the police academy on his own merits. All the other police officers get along well with Sam. I think when the current chief of police retires, the mayor will appoint Sam as the new Chief of Police."

"Which one of the officers who was here is the Chief of Police?" asked Beulah.

Claire explained, "Chief Sorbonne is bedside with his wife. She has terminal cancer."

"I don't know what I would do if something were to happen to Tony."

While the two women visited, Margo and Tony kept up with all the orders that were coming into the kitchen. Suddenly, Tony collapsed to the kitchen floor next to the dishwasher. When Margo screamed, Beulah ran into the kitchen. Claire and Officer Carpenter ran into the kitchen. Bud and Irene ran behind them. Beulah grabbed hold of Tony and brought him to her side. Hysterically, she yelled, "Oh God, not now—not now! Someone call an ambulance, please hurry!"

"Don't call an ambulance," Tony insisted, as Bud Silverman and a male student helped Tony to his feet.

Margo called the Bed and Breakfast to tell Ethan to come to the restaurant. Jake was with Ethan when they came into the kitchen through the back door of the restaurant.

Bud Silverman asked Ethan, "Who's this guy?"

"My cousin, Jake," is all Ethan said as he hugged Margo to his side. When Jake winked at Margo, she blushed and held Ethan closer to her.

Bud Silverman glanced around the kitchen. Many of the students stood around, waiting for directions. Bud, being the military man he was, began to issue directions for cleaning up the restaurant and the kitchen.

In all this commotion, Ethan saw Jake walk out of the back door of the restaurant.

Bud looked around at the students and said, proudly, "I've washed a lot of dishes in my day." Bud grabbed a dry cloth and handed it to one of the students. "It's your job to wipe down all the stainless steel."

Bud's wife, Irene, was out in the restaurant along with other students, wiping down tables. Irene loved working alongside those students.

Margo and Ethan took Tony up to his apartment over the restaurant. Tony assured them he would be fine in the morning.

It was late in the evening when Margo and Ethan inspected the dining room and kitchen. Margo gathered the students around her. She thanked them for their work. She told the students that they were entitled to a free dinner of their choice whenever they wished.

Chapter 14

It was in the springtime when azaleas, crocuses, and apple and plum trees came to life. One late spring day Ethel Freeman received notice that her husband, Arnold, was killed in action. Ethel and Morgan, her son, stood beside her when a Marine honor guard handed Ethel a folded American flag, removed respectfully from atop Arnold's coffin and handed it reverently to Ethel. A bugler played taps while nine of the other Marine honor guards fired a three-gun salute into the air.

Morgan took over the family business while Ethel watched over him to make sure he knew what he was doing. Eventually she retired from the business and went home to live a life of seclusion. Grief-stricken, Ethel died one afternoon in her bed where she had gone to nap.

Ethel's funeral was attended by many people who had come into her jewelry store to purchase high school graduation rings. It was the same jeweler where Ethan purchased the promise ring for Margo. Morgan, at the First Christian Reformed Church, gave a eulogy of his mother and father. Ethan and Beulah were there to pay their respects as were Gary and Heather Souls.

Ethel was buried in the plot next to where her husband, Arnold, had been laid to rest at the Monumenta Cemetery. Jake, Ethan's adopted cousin, was there, too, off in a distant row of graves, inconspicuous to many except Ethan, who bristled at the sight of him and while he wished Jake dead, he had no idea how prophetic his thoughts were.

By late spring, Ethel's funeral was a distant memory to the town of Covington. It was the last day of spring, hot and humid, the right kind of stuff that would produce corn fields six feet tall in the autumn of the year. With graduation just around the corner, Beulah remembered her promise to buy a graduation ring for Ethan. She and Ethan went to Ethel's Fine Jewelry to buy the ring.

Beulah asked Morgan, "Are you going to change the name of your business?"

"No," Morgan replied. I want to keep it in memory of my mother."

Ethan looked at Morgan and said, "Thank you. Every time I look at this ring I'll think of you and your mom."

Morgan gave Beulah a quizzical look and then remarked, "My father bought a grand concert piano as a wedding gift for Mom. Every holiday, birthdays or family get-togethers Mom would play the piano. She taught herself to read music." He paused momentarily and then told Beulah, "I want to gift the piano to you."

Beulah questioned, "How would I get it to the bed and breakfast?"

"A friend of mine owns a moving company. I'll hire him to bring the piano over."

"I'll pay for the move."

"It's a gift from my family to you," Morgan insisted.

For the first time in Beulah's life she was at a loss for words. Tears welled up in her eyes as she looked at Ethan and said, "Let's go home."

Chapter 15

It was the middle of a late spring morning when Beulah sat at the breakfast nook, enjoying a cup of black coffee with a day-old walnut-raisin muffin. Ethan and Margo would be over soon to help Beulah get all the bedrooms and bathrooms ready for the day.

Beulah, with Tony's help, would take care of the living and dining room, kitchen, wash closet, mudroom and entry way. A concert grand piano was now the focal point of the living room. The piano sat in one corner of the room next to six windows that were in an L-shape formation which gave view of the front yard.

By ten Tony and Margo would leave to get the Peking Duck open for lunch and dinner. Ethan would follow an hour later.

After Ethan left, Beulah went into the kitchen to prepare a dozen cinnamon-apple and blueberry muffins for the day. While she prepared the muffins for baking, she listened to music from the local radio station on her cathedral radio that sat on the kitchen counter across from the stove. Soon the station played "Amazing Grace," which was one of Beulah's favorite songs. She never attended church but she considered herself to be a spiritual person. Lost in the moment she closed her eyes and began to hum the song. When she heard the front door open, she removed her apron and walked into the living room. There in front of her stood a man who was dressed in corduroy trousers and brown shirt. He was clean shaven. His cologne was musk. She identified the cologne as the same as Julius, her father, wore.

The man carried a brown suitcase with him.

"May I help you?" Beulah asked.

"My name is Lawrence Depew. I would like a room for a week, maybe longer, until I find a small home in the area. I don't know where to start. I have identification and money." Lawrence sat his suitcase down on the living room floor. He removed his wallet from his back pocket showed his driver's license to Beulah.

Lawrence put his driver's license back in his back pocket.

Beulah said, "I had a couple cancel their reservation this morning. Why don't you come into the kitchen and sit at the breakfast nook? I need to bake a dozen cinnamon-apple and blueberry muffins. It won't take long for me to finish what I started."

"You're a baker?" Lawrence asked as he followed Beulah into the kitchen. He sat his suitcase on the floor next to the breakfast nook and then sat down there.

Beulah began, “I run the bed and breakfast. I have three other helpers. The coffee’s fresh.”

“I would love a cup of coffee, cream if you have some.”

“Tell me more about yourself,” Beulah said as she sat a cup of coffee on the breakfast nook table in front of Lawrence.

“Beverly, my wife, and I farmed north of here. We were best friends since kindergarten.” Lawrence sipped his coffee, then he continued. “I kissed her and told her that she was going to be my wife. I wrapped a piece of my mom’s blue skein around her ring finger. We both told our parents about the blue skein. They thought it was a *phase* we were going through. By the time were in fifth grade, our parents came to realize that I loved Beverly. In senior high my mom gave me her mother’s engagement ring. That night both families got together for dinner at my home and that’s when I put the engagement ring on Beverly’s finger.” Lawrence leaned back into the bench and closed his eyes. “I am so tired that I could fall asleep right here. I have a story to tell you.”

Beulah suggested, “Why don’t you go upstairs to your bedroom. Lie down for a while. I need to get this baking done. When you are rested, come on down. My muffins should be done baking by then and you can tell me your story.”

An hour later the smells of freshly baked cinnamon-apple and blueberry muffins filled the bed and breakfast. These were memories for Beulah of when she lived in San Diego and when she and Lloyd stayed in the bed and breakfast there. Each morning the smell of fresh muffins of all kinds greeted guests to a breakfast of coffee and muffins of their choice. The aroma of those freshly baked muffins woke Lawrence and he came down into the kitchen.

"Are you rested?" Beulah asked Lawrence.

To Beulah's amazement she watched as Lawrence yawned, stood on his tip toes and stretched his arms above his head. Then he bent over and touched the floor with his hands, stood up and twisted his body first to the right and then to the left. After his gymnastics were finished, he sat down at the breakfast nook table.

Eyes wide open Beulah looked at Lawrence and said, "My goodness I got tired just by watching you!"

"Beverly and I used to go for runs around our home just as the sun peeked over the horizon." Tears welled up in his eyes as he said, "I loved her so much."

Softly, Beulah said, "I'm so sorry for your loss."

Lawrence wiped the sleepers from his eyes with a handkerchief from his trouser pocket and then put the handkerchief back into his trouser pocket. He wrapped his hands around the cup of coffee Beulah had sat in front of him. She placed a cinnamon-apple and blueberry muffin on a small dish on the breakfast nook table. Shortly Beulah sat down on the breakfast nook bench across from Lawrence. She smiled at him and said, "Tell me your story."

"I took out an insurance policy for me, to take care of funeral expenses and such in case I passed way before Beverly. A month ago, Beverly collapsed to the floor just as we were sitting down to supper. Our family farm had two giant weeping willows, one on the north side and one on the south side that shielded us from the sizzling summer months. A windmill towered over our home that provided us with some of the most pristine water in the area. The kitchen was the heart of our home and still was. I could take you there and show you around that old house."

"The depression never affected us. We had milk cows, pigs, and a large chicken coop. Mom planted a huge garden each year—potatoes, sweet corn, carrots, lettuce, cabbage and a host of other vegetables."

"Dad sold corn that would be milled into flour and corn meal at the local Co-Op. With the money he made, he bought more corn seed to plant crops for the coming year and flour so Mom could bake all the bread, cookies, and cakes we had during the year. The flour bags had colorful images printed on them. Mom, when she went to town with Dad, would buy a copy of the Sears & Roebuck Company catalogue. The catalogue had all sorts of patterns to make an assortment of clothing. Mom had an old treadle sewing machine that belonged to my grandmother, Olive Bacon."

"My grandmother never approved of Mom's marriage to my father because she wanted Mom to marry a man of money. Her husband, the grandfather I never knew, was a successful banker, a well-respected man in the community. When the depression hit, grandfather lost his bank, his home and all their possessions. Grandpa took his life soon after. My mom never talked about grandfather."

"Grandma Bacon came to live with us shortly after grandpa died. Grandma was a tall, thin woman in frail health. She had terrible loss of memory and there were times when she would walk aimlessly about our house and talk to herself. Sometimes she would go outside and wander about in the corn fields. She would caress a stalk of corn and talk to it as though Grandpa Bacon were there. Mom would find grandma, sitting on the ground between rows of corn, sobbing. Mom was always there for her to comfort her. Mom loved grandma deeply but that love was never given back to Mom because grandma never approved of her marriage to my father, a farmer."

"I have other memories of living on our farm, mostly good. If there were any bad memories in my adult years, I have forgotten all of them. My parents loved one another deeply. I have no memories of them ever arguing."

"On Sundays after church, my father sat at the dining room table reading the morning newspaper that he had picked up in town before we came home. I helped Mom prepare the dinner, chickens in a roasting pan along with an assortment of vegetables."

"Grandma, dinner is on the table," Mom called out.

"After several seconds of silence, Mom walked into the living room. Grandma was a silver-haired, grand old lady who lost her way many times. 'Amnesia,' Mom called Grandma's condition. In her younger days, she played the church piano and sang in the church choir. 'Amazing Grace' was her favorite song and she play that song every Sunday either at church or when she came home from church. She had a beautiful tenor voice back then. As the years passed, her singing voice faded and she had a tough time playing the piano because crippling arthritis ripped through her body, especially her fingers. Her hands and fingers were all shriveled up. They looked like long sticks with bulging nodules on them."

"Mom told me to go outside to find grandma. I did not hear anything at first because a warm summer wind blew to the south around and behind the house. I stepped off the front porch and began to walk around the south side of the house. I stopped dead in my tracks when there in front of me stood grandma singing 'Amazing Grace' to all the chickens in the chicken coop.

She held a willow branch in her right hand as she called out to the chickens—each chicken had a name."

"You are off key," she told one of the chickens. To another she admonished, "Sit tall and straight."

"I was so mesmerized in that moment that I did not notice when Mom walked up to grandma. As she put her arms around grandma's shoulder, grandma looked at her, sobbing she said, "They've all lost their way, like me."

"Just then a huge cock squawked loudly. Grandma pointed to the cock, 'Brian, we've had enough practice for one day.'"

"Mom told me later that Brian was Grandpa Bacon's first name." Lawrence finished his coffee. He looked at Beulah and said, "I need to find a home here."

Beulah handed the *Covington Banner* that was sitting on the counter next to the telephone. "Properties are listed for sale. Bud and Irene Silverman just bought a home." She added quickly, "They stayed here for a while."

Lawrence's eyes opened wide as he said, "Oh, my god! Bud and I were neighbors. He lived a mile from my home. He always told me that he wanted to go into the military when he graduated from high school."

"He did," Beulah said.

Fondly Lawrence said, "When we were boys, Bud and I would go to Rose Creek and fish for hours." He laughed loudly. "I taught him how to put a worm on a fishing hook! I remember when he came to my home and said goodbye and that he was enlisting into the Navy." Sadly, Lawrence added, "I never saw him again."

"I'm sure he would like to see you again," Beulah said and then added, "Call him. Irene, his wife, would like to meet you, too. They are a terrific couple."

"Do you know people who live in the area?" Lawrence asked.

"I do my grocery shopping in town and visit with the merchants I do business with. I stop by the Peking Duck for dinner before I come home."

"Do you know a fellow by the name of Jake Covington?"

Beulah stood flabbergasted, "Why do you ask that?"

"Jake came by my home. He had a burlap bag slung over his shoulder. I never asked him what was in that bag.

"He looked like a gypsy. He helped me clean up the property. I fed him. He seemed like a nice fellow. After I paid him for his work, he left. Never saw him again."

"I have nothing nice to say about Jake. I think it best you forget about him, too."

Chapter 16

Sarah's Bed and Breakfast was full of guests, some local but others who had read the advertisement that Heather Souls had sent to *Sunset Magazine* about the bed and breakfast and had never been to a Midwest town before with its flag-lined streets.

Covington had a milliner and a haberdashery. Myron's grocery had meat lockers for rent in the back of the store as well as an ice house for those who did not have the modern refrigerator with freezers. The red sandstone courthouse had a clock on top that faced north, south, east, and west chimed on each hour. The courthouse housed the police department. A jail was in the basement of the courthouse. Gary and Heather Souls' *Covington Banner* sat next to the police department. James Thornton General Hospital sat on the street across from the police department. James Thornton was a highly decorated field medic and an aide to Teddy Roosevelt when his rough riders charged up San Juan Hill, a decisive battle of the Spanish-American war.

In the fall of the year, Hutterites who lived in colonies nearby would come to town to sell their fall harvests. They had a grocery store of their own that sold honey, flours for baking, as well as quilts made out in the colony and many handmade items such as Conestoga covered wagons made in exquisite detail and a chuck wagon or field kitchen as they were sometimes called. There were a variety of restaurants that sold buttermilk biscuits smothered in sausage gravy, sausage, ham with bacon, eggs and toast with plenty of coffee.

Tony's Peking Duck was a tremendous success fueled by returning veterans who had acquired a taste for Asian food while they served in the South Pacific. Tony taught Ethan how to prepare and serve his signature dish of Peking Duck, mostly the skin and little meat, sliced in front of the diners. The front of the menu read: *Our ducks are bred specially for this dish and are slaughtered after sixty-five days and seasoned before being roasted in an oven. The meat is eaten with spring onion, cucumber, and sweet bean sauce with pancake rolled around the fillings and pork fried or white rice.*

Toad Lake was the anchor for the town of Covington. Signs were placed around the lake that read: **No alcoholic beverages allowed.** The lake was an enormous body of water that was fed from underground streams. It was shaped like a spoon. The shallow end was for swimmers. Thick vegetation grew around the edges of the lake that was home to frogs, toads, and tadpoles. Every Fourth of July as well as on New Year's Eve, frog legs were served along with a variety of casseroles, cookies, pies and cakes. Horseshoes were played along with tugs o' war. Tall logs stacked in the shape of a cone provided a bonfire during the evening hours. The bonfire became a tradition established many years before by Barney Covington and his sons. Now other men in the town took over the tradition. There was a fireworks display, which ended in singing the national anthem. During the winter months when the lake was frozen over, fishermen populated the lake. They drilled holes in the thick ice to drop their lures into the frigid water. Ice skaters took advantage of the frozen lake, too, but they skated at a distance away from the anglers.

Ethan and Margo went out to the lake during the holidays but it was not the same as before when Sarah was there.

One evening while Ethan and Margo stood by the shores of the lake, Ethan turned Margo to face him. He reached into his trouser pocket, pulled out the promise ring box, and opened it so she could see the ring. Ethan dropped down on one knee and asked Margo, "Will you marry me? I know I must finish high school. The only job I've ever had is working in your dad's restaurant." Ethan stood up and placed the promise ring on Margo's left ring finger. "I fell in love with you the first day we met."

Margo as she kissed him said, "Me, too."

The following day when Tony noticed the ring on Margo's finger, he looked at it for a moment and then said to Ethan, "I've always thought of you as my son."

Tears welled up in Ethan's eyes because that was the nicest comment Tony ever made to him.

Margo socked Ethan when she said to Tony, "We want two children, a boy and a girl."

Tony grinned at Ethan as he said, "I know who's going to wear the pants in this family."

Ethan slept in Sarah's home. It would always be Sarah's home no matter where his life's travels took him. Margo slept in her bedroom in the upstairs apartment above the Peking Duck. They were careful not to be too intimate because they did not believe in sex before marriage.

Chapter 17

As graduation was coming soon, Ethan sat with Bud on the davenport in the living room of the Bed and Breakfast to talk about his future. Bud asked Ethan how his grades were. Ethan responded, "I have all A's except for one A minus." He explained further, "Margo helped me a lot with algebra. I got good grades in chemistry and physics, too. I excelled in astronomy in school. When I was a kid, I told my dad that someday men would walk on the moon and travel to Mars. I have a lot of Buck Rogers and Flash Gordon magazines stored in a pine box in the bedroom of my home. I used to read them in the evening while my father read the newspaper." He paused to focus on the present as he asked, "Why did you become a hospital corpsman?"

"I was born and raised on a farm not far from here. One spring day my father had an accident in the barn. I remember my mom running into the kitchen to ask for help. She grabbed the receiver off the phone that was mounted on the wall next to the icebox. My mom told me one time that if I ever had to use the phone to be careful as to what I said because the phone was on a party line. I watched as she held the receiver to her ear and rapidly turned the crank on the opposite side of the phone."

"I don't remember how long it took the doctor to get there but I do remember that he saved my father's life. In that moment, I wanted to be a doctor. I didn't have money to go to medical school. I remember the day the Navy recruiter came to our high school. After his presentation was over, I walked up to the recruiter and told him that I wanted to be a doctor like the doctor who saved my dad's life."

Bud sat down at the breakfast nook across from Ethan who noticed a brass plate with his name etched on top of the cedar box. A drawer was located at the bottom of the box. Inside the box was a china plate and bell of Norman Rockwell's *Looking Out to Sea*. Bud lifted the plate and bell out of the box and set them on top of the breakfast nook in front of Ethan. He slid open the drawer and pulled out a beige envelope. He removed the card inside the envelope and handed it to Ethan and as he did this, he told Ethan, "Irene gave this box and its contents to me as a wedding gift. She told me that you should have the box to remember us by when you go into the Navy. We have grown quite fond of you in the brief time we have known you."

Old Sailor

**Come and sit beside the ships, Old Sailor,
And all your dreams release,
And in all the noise, of this busy dock
Somehow, you'll find peace;
You'll toss aside the bygone years
And dream of battles old,
You'll see the captain at the helm
So, daring and so bold
You'll see brave men at battle stations
Fighting till they die
You'll look up and see the stars and stripes
And the sea gulls in the sky
And while you're sitting beside the ships
You'll smell the salty air
You'll feel the mist upon your face
While wind blows through your hair
You'll feel so young again, somehow,
You'll wear a child's smile
Through all the pains of aging life
You'll be content for awhile
But, now it's getting late Old Sailor
The dock is quiet and still
The sea is calm, the ships are moored
The wind begins to chill
Now, it's time to leave the sea
Return to the realm of men
To get the rest that you will need,
To come and dream again.**

Ethan was so taken aback by Bud and Irene's gift that for a moment, he sat there unable to speak. Finally, he said, "Thank you."

Bud told Ethan to come down to the recruiting station the following day after school and that he would give him a series of tests to see if Ethan qualified to be a doctor. Bud was astonished when he graded the examination Ethan had taken because he scored a 98 out of 100. Bud talked to Ethan about the hospital corpsman rating. Ethan knew in his soul that that is what he wanted to do.

Chapter 18

An hour had passed since the Peking Duck closed.

Ethan pulled the bamboo window shades down and then he locked the front door. The dining room staff watched as he inspected the dining room. Ethan looked under the tables and chairs for gum that had been stuck there by patrons who had come into the restaurant to eat the lunch or dinner meal. He noted with pleasure that the dining room staff had cleaned them thoroughly. He thanked them all for a job well done and sent them home through the rear door of the eatery.

Each kitchen staff was responsible for a work station and once their work was done, Margo inspected their station and thanked them for all the diligent work they had done. Margo unlocked the rear door to let the kitchen staff out and then she locked the back door behind them.

Ethan brought two tills over to Margo. She counted the tills at the end of the day. The overages were rubber banded together and dropped into a safe that was in Tony's office. Margo and Tony were the only ones who had a key to that safe. Now in his senior year Ethan made several deposits to the Covington

Mercantile. When Ethan returned, he and Margo sat at the round table diagonally from the front door of the Peking Duck.

Ethan sat back in his wooden chair and closed his eyes. Margo dotted his brow with a napkin she pulled off from the wheeled cart that had all the condiments and napkins on it.

Margo had graduated from Lewis and Clark High the previous year. When Ethan took her hand in his, he looked at Margo and asked, "You were the valedictorian of your class. What did you talk about?"

Margo said, "I talked about Tony and why I loved him so much. How I wish I had known my mom."

In Ethan's freshman year there was a measure on the city ballot that asked voters to change Covington High to Lewis and Clark High. The voters approved the recommendation by an overwhelming majority. The high school opened in the spring of 1893. It was four stories high with turrets on each corner of the roof. The building resembled a medieval castle and made of smoked sand stone. The school was a source of pride to the older generation, but the younger generation thought it to be an eye sore and ought to be torn down to be replaced by a more modern structure. This would happen while Ethan was in naval training center San Diego, California. Margo would write a letter to him about the old school's demise.

* * *

Margo, Tony, and Beulah were in the auditorium the day Ethan graduated from high school. Tony had closed the restaurant so they could celebrate Ethan's graduation. Ethan and Margo would never forget this day for years to come.

The crowd stood up and cheered as Ethan walked up the podium. He was as sure of himself as he had ever been in his long life.

"I am Ethan Covington. It is an honor for me to stand before you today as the valedictorian of the class of 1953. I need to acknowledge our high school principal and all the high school administrative staff here today. We—my classmates seated before me and I—are about to cross over a threshold into our unknown future—but I believe in all of you." Applause. "We walk this way only once so I want all of you to make the most of each day as if it were your last."

Ethan named one of his classmates who died of cancer. He noted how all his class attended the funeral, six were pall bearers. Tears were wept that day as classmates held on to one another followed by the class song. Afterward a remembrance of the young man's life was held in the high school gymnasium. He played football, track, and baseball well. His walk reflected a man who was secure within himself and he was a gorgeous young man. His hair was in a butch cut. He wore his letterman jacket proudly but not in a narcissistic sense. High school girls swooned over him but he kept their advances at an arm's length, telling all those girls that he would give his body to the woman he would marry. In the class drama department, he acted well and had a beautiful tenor voice and was animated on stage.

Ethan said of him, "He would have been your class valedictorian had he lived."

Ethan continued. "I am about to enter military service. I want to thank Bud Silverman, my Navy recruiter and friend, for his advice about the Naval service. I want to be a combat hospital corpsman and serve with Marines like he did."

Ethan looked at Margo as he said, "My wife-to-be, soon."

His classmates stood up as they chanted, "Margo, Margo, Margo! Is there a preacher in the house?"

A hush fell over his classmates as Ethan motioned them to sit back down.

"Just wish us well," Ethan said. "In closing I want to wish all of you the best for the future as you embark on your next journey. In another year and every year after that, we can all come back here to see how much we have changed."

One of the graduating students called out, "When's the wedding?"

"Margo and I will be married in Grace Episcopalian Church tomorrow afternoon at one. Our wedding reception will be held at the Peking Duck. Margo's father owns the restaurant. If you've never had Chinese food before, I encourage you go give Tony's place a visit."

Later on that graduation day, Ethan returned to the Peking Duck with Margo for dinner and to talk about their wedding plans. Tony's staff had already decorated the dining room with balloons and a poster that wished the newlyweds well. Beulah had taken Ethan and Margo to a shop in town a week before that specialized in men's tuxedos and wedding gowns. Beulah paid for Ethan's tuxedo and Margo's wedding dress.

Beulah's parents, Julius and Tami, were devout Episcopalians. Beulah and Lloyd were active members, too. After Lloyd was killed during his training accident, Beulah stopped going to church. She was like a ship without a rudder in stormy seas. Ethan had been brought up in the Episcopalian Church by his mother. After Sarah died, Beulah encouraged Ethan to go to church even though she did not attend herself.

Chapter 19

The day after graduation found everyone at Grace Episcopal Church.

Wedding menu cards were given out to everyone who attended the wedding ceremony as they entered the church.

Ethan looked stunning dressed in his tuxedo and boutonniere. Margo wore Beulah's wedding gown with a corsage wrapped around her wrist. Beulah had taken her wedding dress with Margo to Amy's Alterations who tailored Beulah's dress to fit Margo.

Ethan had asked Bud Silverman to be his best man. Margo had asked Irene Silverman to be her matron of honor.

Beulah had given her engagement ring to Margo. Beulah had taken Ethan and Margo to Ethel's Fine Jewelry to purchase a wedding ring for Margo and one for Ethan, too.

Gary and Heather Souls were there and Heather was the official photographer for the wedding.

The church was filled with people who had either stayed at Sarah's Bed and Breakfast or had read Beulah's advertisement that appeared in *Sunset Magazine*. Many had dined at the Peking

Duck. Tony owned a laundry mat that serviced linens to the hospital and other businesses who had need of linens.

Miriam and Tyler Moore, her husband, attended the wedding. Officer Carpenter and Claire were there. Nora Pullman sent an arrangement of flowers and a check for Ethan and Margo.

Ethan stood in front of the church next to his best man and the minister. Everyone stood to look at the rear of the church as the organist played Mendelssohn's wedding march. Four young flower girls followed behind Irene Silverman, Margo's matron of honor, and one of them carried a wedding pillow with wedding rings on them. Slowly Tony walked Margo down the aisle to where Ethan stood. Margo's face was veiled.

Beulah's eyes became teary as she thought how proud Sarah and Andrew would be of Ethan.

The minister looked at Margo and Ethan as he said, "Repeat after me. I, Ethan Covington, take you, Margo Wong, to be my wife, to have and to hold from this day forward, for better or for worse, for richer, for poorer, in sickness and in health, to love and to cherish, from this day forward until death do us part." Margo repeated her vows and then the minister said, "You may kiss the bride."

Ethan lifted the veil off Margo's face and said, "I love you so much." And then he kissed Margo.

They turned to face the congregation as they began to walk down the aisle toward the entry to the church. Once outside, throngs of people tossed rice over Margo and Ethan.

Beulah had loaned them her car to drive that had tin cans tied to the rear bumper and letters painted over the rear window that read: *Just married.* Beulah had loaned Margo and Ethan her apartment over the garage for them to stay for their honeymoon.

Beulah would ask Tony to marry her after Margo and Ethan's wedding. She had resisted the marriage before because she thought that if she married Tony, they would not be friends anymore but now that was a silly notion to her.

* * *

The town of Covington was a patriotic town. In the Twilight Nursing Home lived a 93-year-old Civil War veteran who was in frail physical condition, but his mind was sharp. He remembered the time he met president Abraham Lincoln. He was a cook in a mess tent when the President stepped inside to have lunch with the enlisted men.

Because Covington was a patriotic town with its flag-lined streets, most family members had a son or father in their family who had served in World War II. They talked to their sons about the draft that was in process. Those sons had some knowledge of the likelihood of being drafted and when their draft notice would be received, but until the draft notices were received, they could choose to enlist and take advantage of training or career field guarantees by one of the military services.

When Ethan was at the beginning of his senior, year recruiters from Army, Navy, Air Force, Marines and National Guards came to Lewis and Clark High School's auditorium to talk to the senior students about what each service had to offer them. The recruiters were all in full dress uniform and had brought with them colorful brochures that advertised what each service had to offer recruits.

When Ethan graduated and lost his student deferment, his local draft board called him in to receive his reclassification notice to category 1-A for the draft. Ethan was told that he could expect to receive his draft notice in the mail within 60 days. Unofficially, the secretary of the draft board said that most draftees were going to the combat arms of the Army and Marine Corps. The next day, Ethan had called Bud Silverman and told him that he was going to receive his draft notice.

Ethan had scored in the 95th percentile on his proactive examination. An hour later Bud Silverman had Ethan take the second and final examination to see if his first aptitude examination was accurate and it was.

The Monday after Ethan graduated from high school, Bud Silverman had Ethan come into his office.

Ethan raised his right hand to take his oath of enlistment. Margo, Tony, Beulah, and Gary and Heather Souls were there.

Ethan's photograph appeared on the front page of the *Covington Banner* the following day. Margo and Beulah would each keep a copy of that issue in her cedar chest. Tony placed copies on the front counter of the Peking Duck.

The following Monday morning Ethan climbed aboard the Greyhound bus bound for San Diego, California, and eventually to the Naval recruit training base.

Chapter 20

One late summer morning the telephone rang just as Beulah got out of bed. She stood on her tiptoes next to her bed and stretched her arms above her head. As she lifted the receiver to her ear, she greeted the caller drowsily, "Sarah's Bed and Breakfast."

The familiar voice on the other end caught Beulah off guard. For a moment, she hesitated and then questioned, "Miriam, is that you?"

"It is," Miriam said. "How is the bed and breakfast coming along?"

Beulah said, "Business was slow at first, but it is beginning to pick up."

Miriam continued "Tyler Moore, my husband, works for a large airline. We would like to spend Thanksgiving this year at Sarah's Bed and Breakfast. Will you be open?"

"Sarah's Bed and Breakfast is open year around." Beulah began as she opened her appointment calendar to November. "We're booked up with returning guests over the Thanksgiving holiday weekend, but you and Tyler can stay in my apartment above the garage."

"If you give us your apartment, where will you sleep?"

"I'll be with Tony. He lives in an apartment above the restaurant."

"How is Tony? He has a daughter but I don't remember her name."

"Margo is his daughter's name."

Beulah could tell by Miriam's voice that she was not the same woman she once knew when Miriam was married to Luke Covington.

"Oh, yes, I remember now. Would you mind if my sister Marsha and Evan, her husband, come along with us?" she asked, and then added in a caring tone of voice, "It will be good to see you again."

Beulah said, "I'll make a note of it and if a room becomes available, I'll let you know. If not at Thanksgiving, perhaps Marsha and Evan could come another time," she paused and then added, "I have one of Norman Rockwell's plates of a small Midwestern town hanging on my wall in the living room. Guests tell me when they see that plate that it reminds them of Covington in the summer months. You remember that Toad Lake isn't far from here, a good place for you and Tyler to swim or fish or picnic."

"We'll have a memorable Thanksgiving," Beulah said, "Do you remember Officer Carpenter?"

"I do. Why do you ask?"

"Officer Carpenter was here a few months ago. He told me that his office had received a request from Jake's probation officer saying Jake would like to return to Covington. He wanted to ask Ethan's forgiveness for what he did to him. Jake is somewhere around here. What do you think?"

Miriam said, her voice strained, shaken, "Jake represents a part of my life that I would just as soon forget." She fell silent for a moment, and then said, "I'll have to talk to my priest about Jake."

Beulah asked, "How did you find Jake?"

Miriam queried, "Why do you want to know?"

"I would like to find out some background information about Jake, where he was born, who his mom and dad were—that kind of stuff."

Miriam cautioned, "I don't know where you would begin to get that information. Adoption records are sealed, aren't they?"

"I think if you know the right person, you can get information you need to know about anyone."

"Knowing you, as I do…," Miriam's voice fell silent as she hung up her receiver.

Beulah looked at her receiver, wondering, *what was that all about?*

Beulah had just hung up the receiver when the telephone rang again.

"Sarah's Bed and Breakfast." When there was no answer, Beulah repeated herself. She was about to hang up the receiver when she heard a woman's voice sobbing on the other end.

"Who is this?" Beulah asked sharply.

Faintly the woman said, "This is Nora Pullman."

Goosebumps immediately formed on Beulah's arms when she asked, "Edgar?"

"Edgar died in his sleep last night."

"Oh, my," Beulah said. "I am sorry for your loss."

"We had a good fifty-seven years of marriage. He was a good husband and provider. The mortgage to our home has been paid off for some time now. I am surrounded by wonderful friends who are like family to me."

Beulah was thoughtful for a moment. "Do you read the *Covington Banner*? I remember Gary telling me that you were on his mailing list."

"I look forward to receiving it each month. I want to thank you for the hospitality you extended to Edgar and me."

"Write me a letter when you have time?"

Nora said, "Edgar was the letter writer. I have to go now." And she hung up the receiver.

"Goodbye to you, too," Beulah said as she hung up her receiver.

Moments later Gary Souls arrived at the Bed and Breakfast.

Beulah said, "I just spoke to Miriam! It was good to hear her voice. Then Nora Pullman called to tell me that Edgar died in his sleep." Beulah had a sudden flash of insight as she looked at Gary and said, "You know everybody in this town, don't you?"

"No. I don't know everybody."

"Do you know a Patricia Marr?"

"I don't, but Heather does. They've been best friends since third grade."

As Gary telephoned Heather, he looked at Beulah and said, "I came over for a cup of coffee."

"I baked oatmeal-walnut muffins with raisins earlier this morning. How about a muffin with your coffee?"

"That would be wonderful," Gary said as he removed a notepad and pencil from his shirt pocket. He scribbled a telephone number Heather gave him on the notepad and as he did this Beulah called out, "Thank you, Heather."

"You're welcome," Beulah heard Heather say.

Gary ripped the note from the notepad and handed it to Beulah. "Do you think Patricia Marr will talk to me?"

"We'll soon find out," Gary said as he picked up the telephone receiver and dialed the number to Patricia's home. Shortly a female's voice came over the telephone. After Gary talked to Patricia for a few minutes, he handed the receiver to Beulah.

When Beulah explained to Patricia why she wanted to talk to her, Patricia told her she was free for the rest of the afternoon. "I'm willing to come over to your place to discuss this with you personally," she offered.

Beulah accepted.

Gary washed the remainder of the oatmeal-walnut muffin down with the last swallow of coffee. He set the coffee cup down, looked at Beulah and said, "Thank you."

"You're welcome," Beulah said and then asked, "What are you and Heather doing for Thanksgiving? I'd love to have you both join us for dinner."

"Heather and I are always at the newspaper or out on the town looking for local interest stories." He grinned. "We just might take you up on your Thanksgiving dinner."

Beulah reminisced, "Every Thanksgiving when Sarah was alive, we had Thanksgiving dinner at her house. Miriam was there a few times before she moved to Fallon, Nevada, to be with her sister, Marsha."

"What do you wish us to bring?"

"Does Heather bake pies?"

"I'm the pie and bread baker. How about a pumpkin and a pecan pie?"

"Wonderful," Beulah said. "Tony, Margo, and Ethan will be here, too, along with other guests who have made reservations for that time." Tears welled up in Beulah's eyes as she added, "Memories of Sarah."

Chapter 21

Patricia Marr was a short, stout woman with auburn hair. She was wearing a yellow polka-dot dress and black shoes. She had a birthmark on the left side of her neck.

Beulah invited Patricia to sit on the davenport and offered Patricia coffee and one of her oatmeal-walnut muffins with raisins. Beulah removed the metal box from the fireplace mantel and brought it over to Patricia. "I discovered this metal box in the old garage. I don't know who Rose C. was."

As soon as Patricia opened the metal box tears welled up in her eyes. She looked at Beulah and said, "I had forgotten about Rose."

Patricia began. "When I was a little girl, I remember my parents talking about Rose. I'm sure this is the same woman. She was born with Down syndrome and a cleft palate. She was Joseph Covington's daughter. Joseph was the youngest of Barney Covington's sons. Few of the Covingtons wanted anything to do with Rose because to them, she was a hideous freak of nature." She paused. "There was a man, but I don't know if he was from Covington or not, who befriended her. He pretended to be in love with her, and he gave her a gold engagement ring to profess his love for her. Rose craved affection, physical touch and embrace, and she took this man to her bed. She loved him so much, but that love was never returned and instead he walked out of her life. Nine months later, Rose gave birth to a baby boy. One of the Covingtons—I don't recall who—took the baby to the hospital and left him there. Rose died shortly thereafter of a broken heart."

Sadly, Patricia added, "I don't know whatever became of that baby. No one talked about him." Patricia fell silent for a moment, then she looked at Beulah and said, "I have the ring this fellow gave to Rose, but originally the diamond was missing."

"How did you come into possession of the ring?" Beulah asked.

"My parents had it for a long time. Mom told me that she would take it to a jeweler and have a diamond put in it for me. I agreed to this proposition, but after only a few years, I decided not to wear that ring anymore. You know what? I need to give that ring to you to put in the metal box. I hardly wear it anymore because it reminds me of that poor woman."

Beulah visited with Patricia for a while longer and then in the early afternoon Patricia told Beulah she had errands to run.

The following day Patricia returned to the Bed and Breakfast and gave the engagement ring to Beulah. When Beulah questioned Patricia if this is what she wanted to do, Patricia said,

"My husband gave me a wedding ring he had made for me. I don't need this ring."

Beulah telephoned Gary and Heather Souls to come to the Bed and Breakfast. She had found out who Rose C. was!

Beulah told Gary and Heather they should invite Patricia over for an interview and that the interview would take place at the Beulah's place. The following morning just before lunch, Patricia returned to the Bed and Breakfast along with Gary and Heather.

Patricia and Heather attended the same one-room schoolhouse five miles north of Covington. When they went into the third grade, the new Covington Elementary school opened. They attended the same junior and senior high. Patricia was the high school valedictorian. Heather was the editor of the school newspaper called *The Bulletin.* After Heather graduated, she filled out a job application for work at the *Covington Banner* and went to work the following day as the newspaper reporter. Patricia married a man who worked on the family farm after he graduated. He hated farming and was always looking for better ways to improve his life. A year after he graduated he applied for and got a job working for the Department of Licensing, a state job that provided good income with benefits.

His name was Edwin Benson and this was the first-time Beulah knew Patricia was married to Edwin Benson.

Chapter 22

The following afternoon Edwin Benson stopped by the Bed and Breakfast. He looked at Beulah and said, "I'd like to bring Patricia here over Labor Day weekend. Do you have rooms available during that holiday weekend?"

Beulah glanced over the September register and noted that there was one room left. Suddenly, Beulah realized what was missing in the brochure for Sarah's Bed and Breakfast.

"My goodness," she said as she looked at Edwin.

"Gary Souls showed me the draft of a brochure for Sarah's Bed and Breakfast that he and Heather created. It was an appealing work, but now I know what's missing."

"What was that?" Edwin asked.

Beulah threw her hands in the air like a child who had found her long lost toy.

"The antique crapper that Sarah and I rescued from the barn on the Benson property! Sarah had wanted to learn how to drive, so I took her to the safest place I knew of. I didn't want Sarah to hurt anything." Beulah paused. "I need to have Tony bring that crapper to the Bed and Breakfast. I'll fill it with flowers come spring and put it on the front lawn."

"What is it you want me to do?" Tony asked as he walked into the Bed and Breakfast from the back door."

Beulah looked at Tony and said, "I want you to bring the crapper that is sitting on the front lawn of Sarah's home and put it on the front lawn of the Bed and Breakfast."

"What for?"

Beulah said, emphatically, "It belongs here!"

"Why don't you wait until after the holidays and you aren't so busy?"

Beulah, for most of her life, could get done what she wanted to get done. After all, she was the daughter of a non-commissioned officer in the Marine Corps in San Diego, California. When her father spoke, he got whatever he wanted so Beulah thought that this would carry over to her own life. To her frustration as she acclimated to civilian life, she soon discovered she had to cultivate people around her that she could count on to do what she wanted to get done.

There were times when she wished she was still tucked into the cocoon of military life.

Chapter 23

In the autumn of the year, trees around Covington exploded in a kaleidoscope of magnificent colors. Sights and smells of the coming Thanksgiving feast appeared in grocery stores along with the sounds of Christmas carols. You could feel the excitement in the air as people prepared for the coming holiday season.

It was the day before Thanksgiving when Miriam and Tyler Moore, Miriam's second husband, arrived at Sarah's Bed and Breakfast. Tyler had rented a car after they arrived at the airport from one of the rental car agencies across from the baggage claim area.

They sat with Beulah in the breakfast nook, drinking coffee and enjoying the blueberry muffins Beulah had baked earlier in the morning. Tyler wore corduroy trousers, a shirt, and wing-tip shoes. He had black wavy hair and wore an aviator temperature conversion ring on his right hand. Miriam wore a teal-colored dress with matching jacket and shoes.

Beulah asked Miriam, "What brought you both together?"

Miriam said, "I got a job at the officer's club as a cashier and I waited tables, too, when we were short staffed. One evening

Tyler came into the club for dinner and I happened to be his waitress."

Tyler said, "Miriam's a beautiful woman inside and out. She needed a man in her life who would care for her. She told me about her marriage to Luke. I told her she could be anything she wanted to be. I did not realize how poor of a self-image she had until I got to know her better."

Miriam looked at Beulah and said, "I went back to school and got my GED and went on for an Associate of Arts in liberal arts and then worked for my Bachelors in hotel and motel management." She paused as she looked at Tyler and said, "I am a different person now because of him."

It was near midnight when Miriam said to Beulah, "We need to go to bed."

When Miriam offered to do the dishes, Beulah told her to leave them alone—the dishes could wait until the following morning,

During the night, an autumn storm covered the old snow that had fallen on the first of November. The following morning as the sun rose over clear skies, families created a variety of snowmen with carrots for noses, buttons for eyes and pitch forks or straw brooms thrust deep into the snowmen while other snowmen had hats on the tops of their heads.

Miriam and Tyler were up before dawn. Miriam made a pot of coffee and put out an assortment of muffins Beulah had baked the day before. Tyler washed the dishes that had been left in the kitchen sink overnight.

Beulah came down to the kitchen just as Tyler finished drying the dishes. "Thank you," she said to Tyler.

"I was a bachelor all my life until I met Mariam."

During the night, Ethan had arrived on a bus from California and he went straight to the Peking Duck. Margo and Tony had waited up for him. For Margo, these past months seemed like years.

The next morning Tony brought over three six-foot rectangular tables from the Peking Duck with Margo and Ethan's help. Beulah was overjoyed to see Ethan. She kissed and hugged him tightly for Ethan was the son she never had. She stepped back to give Ethan a once over. Gone were his undisciplined adolescent looks that were replaced by his military bearing. His hair was cut short as were his side burns. He wore his dress military uniform proudly. The caduceus on his right arm signified that he was a Navy medic. He wore the Marine Corps medical indicating that he is now a Navy combat medic serving with the Marines like Bud Silverman.

Then Beulah introduced Miriam and Tyler to Tony and Margo. "Of course, you remember Ethan," Beulah said proudly. Ethan brought over a suitcase with civilian clothes in it. He went up to Beulah's apartment to change and returned to the kitchen.

Miriam washed pots and pans in the kitchen sink without anyone asking her to do so. Tyler helped Tony unfold and set up the rectangular tables while Margo and Beulah prepared the sage stuffing made from dried bread that Beulah saved during the year. Once Margo crumbled up the dried bread, Beulah poured chicken broth she purchased from the grocery store.

Margo and Ethan stuffed, trussed and basted the skin of the turkey with butter, salt, and pepper while Beulah washed and dried the graniteware roasting pan. She placed the stainless-steel roasting rack inside the graniteware roasting pan and set it aside. Margo, while Ethan steadied the roaster, lifted the turkey and placed it in the roasting pan and placed the lid on the roaster. Beulah held open the oven door as Ethan maneuvered the roaster into the oven. After that was done, Beulah emptied a ten-pound bag of potatoes into the kitchen sink. They all peeled, washed and quartered potatoes and placed the potatoes in a stock pot that Beulah had placed on the kitchen counter. Ethan covered the potatoes with water and after that he placed the pot on top of the kitchen stove to boil.

Miriam and Tyler helped Beulah prepare the two rectangular tables that were in the living room. Beulah brought out the Fiesta ware tablecloth and the linen tablecloth that had the whiskey stain on one corner from the china hutch. They set the table with Sarah's fluffy rose and Beulah's Fiesta ware china alternating plates. They placed the dishes one after the other.

Miriam folded napkins in a cone-shaped design and placed them in the crystal drinking glasses in the middle of each plate.

Before noon Gary and Heather arrived with two pumpkin and pecan pies into the Bed and Breakfast. Bud and Irene Silverman arrived a brief time later.

As the other guests arrive during the morning, Ethan is the center of attention. Everyone wanted to know how he likes the Navy and to hear about his experiences in San Diego.

Ethan asks everyone to sit in a circle around him.

He began, "San Diego is a Navy town full of merchants trying to get sailors to spend money in their businesses—from tattoo parlors to businesses that offer lockers for enlisted men to store their civilian clothes. Only officers and senior noncommissioned officers can have civilian clothes in their lockers on board their ships."

"There are restaurants that offer a wide variety foods from around the world—Chinese food," he paused as he nodded to Tony. "I strolled around Chinatown while I was in C school. I missed the Peking Duck because your food is authentic Chinese cuisine." He shrugged his shoulders as he added, "Okay, so I'm partial to your food."

Everyone laughed.

"What is C school?" someone asked.

"C school trains me to become a combat medic so I can be assigned with the Marines," he glanced at Bud Silverman, "like you did. I enlisted for five years so I could go to C school. I was a black belt before I enlisted into the military. I asked Tony, a black belt himself, if he would teach me martial arts. One evening above the Peking Duck Tony began to teach me martial arts. Before that I had no idea how I would protect myself." He paused. "But black belt training won't protect me from a gun."

Beulah interrupted as she looked at Ethan, "Turkey's about ready to come out of the oven."

There would be other days when people would ask Ethan a question or two about his life in the military but for now, Ethan wanted to enjoy the company of his family and friends around the Thanksgiving dinner table.

Beulah had Ethan remove the graniteware roaster from the oven on top of the stove next to the potatoes to see if the turkey was done. When Beulah wiggled one of the drum sticks, it fell out of its joint. She had Ethan return the graniteware roaster to the oven without the roaster lid to brown. Using hot pads, Ethan emptied the steaming water out of the stock pot into the sink. Margo removed butter from the refrigerator while Ethan began mashing potatoes. After the potatoes were mashed, Beulah sat a large Fiesta ware bowl on the sink for the potatoes. While Margo and Ethan emptied the mashed potatoes into the bowl, Beulah opened the oven door for Tony to remove the browned turkey. Tyler steadied the roaster while Tony lifted the turkey out onto a large fluffy rose platter and then removed the stuffing from inside the turkey.

"Let me make the gravy," Miriam said to Beulah. "I've learned how to make good gravy from one of the cooks at the officer's club." Once the gravy was made, Beulah gave her a Fiesta ware blue gravy boat to fill with the gravy.

After all the food was placed on the table, Tony sat at the head of the table with Beulah at the other end of the table. Tyler sat next to Tony while Miriam sat next to Beulah. Ethan and Margo sat in the middle of the table across from one another as did Elsa Meyers and Patricia Marr. Gary and Heather Souls sat across the table from one another.

Tony looked at Tyler and asked, "Would you bless the food, please?"

Tyler began, "Our Father, who art in heaven," and soon everyone said in unison, "hallowed be thy name. Thy Kingdom come, Thy will be done on earth, as it is in heaven. Give us this day our daily bread. And forgive us our trespasses as we forgive them that trespass against us. And lead us not into temptation, but deliver us from evil. For Thine is the kingdom, the power, and the glory, forever and ever. **Amen!**"

During the laughter, storytelling about all the highs and lows of all their lives and the passing of food around the table, Tony reminded Ethan, "Tomorrow you and I will bring our Christmas tree home."

"Mind if I come along?" Tyler asked Tony.

Tony said to Tyler, "You are part of the family now."

After everyone had their fill of the Thanksgiving dinner, Beulah served Gary Souls' pecan and pumpkin pies with a scoop of vanilla ice cream.

Just as Beulah sat down, there was a knock at the front door. When Beulah stood up, Jake walked into the Bed and Breakfast.

Miriam glared at Jake.

Tyler said to Jake, "So you're the black sheep of the family."

Jake ignored Tyler's comment as he asked Beulah, "How come I wasn't invited to Thanksgiving dinner?" He was shabbily dressed in layers of street clothes, a thick red beard and disheveled hair that covered his face. He glared at Ethan and said, "You've always had a family who loved you." He looked at Miriam and said, "Luke loved me more than you ever did."

Tony stood up and walked over to Jake. The two men stood nose-to-nose as Tony said, "If you know what's good for you, you'd better leave."

Miriam cried into Tyler's shoulder as Jake walked out of the Bed and Breakfast.

Beulah looked at Miriam and said, "I had no idea Jake was going to show up. I hope you believe that."

Miriam calmed as she sat up in her chair. She wetted her napkin in her glass of chilly water and then wiped her face with it. She looked at Beulah and said, "I know you didn't."

In the early morning hours, Jake sneaked into the Bed and Breakfast through the back door and on into the living room. He removed the metal box from the fireplace mantel and quietly walked out of the Bed and Breakfast.

Chapter 24

The following morning the smells of the Thanksgiving feast lingered throughout the Bed and Breakfast. Ethan opened the rear door and came into the Bed and Breakfast. Beulah always had a fresh pot of coffee and freshly baked muffins of some kind. This morning she had baked cinnamon apple muffins.

"How do you make these?" Ethan asked as he and Beulah sat down at the breakfast nook.

"I found a basic muffin recipe in the *Covington Banner* under the food section."

"Would you teach me how to make these?" Ethan asked.

Beulah laughed and said, "If I can bake these muffins, anybody can. Let me know when you want to take your baking lessons."

"I love the aroma of freshly baked muffins." Ethan paused as he looked at Beulah and asked, "Do you have brothers or sisters? I don't know anything about your family."

Beulah said, "I was an only child."

"What was your mom's name?"

"Tami. My father's first name is Julius."

"Are you a lot like your mom?"

"More like my dad."

"Do you ever talk to them, I mean since you've been up here?"

"Once a month, maybe more. If I don't call home at least one time, Dad calls me to find out how I am doing."

"Were you married?"

"I was, not for very long, though. My husband was a fighter pilot. He died during a training exercise. I'll never forget that day. Mom and Dad were with me through that whole ordeal. They loved him very much."

"Do you think your parents would like me?"

Beulah reached across the table and squeezed Ethan's hand in her hand as she looked at him and said, affectionately, "Very much so."

Ethan changed the subject when he said, "Why did Jake come back here. I don't trust him."

"You're not alone," Beulah paused. "With Officer Carpenter's help, we'll watch his every move."

After Ethan drank his coffee and ate his muffin, they stood up and hugged one another. He started to walk out when his eye caught sight of the fireplace mantle. His heart skipped a beat when he realized the metal box was gone!

Beulah stood next to him and said, "I'm so used to seeing it there." Goosebumps formed on her arms as a chill rippled through her body.

They both looked at one another and said, in unison, "Jake?"

Beulah immediately called Officer Carpenter and asked him to come to the Bed and Breakfast.

After he walked in, Beulah looked at Officer Carpenter and said, "The metal box is gone and we suspect Jake took it."

"Do you know where he is?"

"No, we don't know where Jake lives."

"The only motel in town is across the street from the Greyhound bus station. He's probably staying there, unless he is staying with friends. So, that's a good starting point," suggested Officer Carpenter.

An hour later Beulah got a telephone call from Officer Carpenter. He told Beulah that he found the metal box, and its contents, strewn about Jake's motel room.

Officer Carpenter put out an All-Points Bulletin to all the police cars in the Covington area.

Residents in and around the town of Covington who owned police scanners set up neighborhood block watches to watch out for Jake.

Meanwhile Officer Carpenter considered all of Jake's options. Would he have gone to a friend's house? If not, then where?

Ethan and Margo were staying at Sarah's house. While the police scoured the neighborhood around Ethan's home, Ethan lay on the brown tweed davenport in the living room. A

Pendleton earth blanket covered his body. Margo had gone to work. He had gone back to bed after she left, but his REM sleep was interrupted when he thought he heard a knock on the front door. He got up, put on his bathrobe and walked out into the living room from the bedroom. He switched on the porch light and looked through the glass of the living room door, but saw no one standing there. He turned off the porchlight and lay back down on the davenport and fell into a light sleep.

Suddenly Ethan caught sight of someone standing at the front door. Ethan got up and turned on the porchlight. It was Jake. Ethan opened the door and invited him in.

"What are you doing here?" Ethan asked.

"I've been up all night, walking around town." Jake lied. A rush of anger began to swell inside of him. "I need someone to talk to."

"Can't it wait until later?"

Jake's body shook as tears welled up in his eyes.

Now, everything Ethan learned through his martial arts and military training told him something was horribly wrong with Jake. Ethan did everything he could to repress his fears.

Jake's stance stiffened, his face tightened, "You think you're so much better than me, don't you?!"

"What the hell are you talking about?"

Jake reached inside his coat pocket and pulled out a piece of paper that had *Rose C.* written on it. Sobbing, he thrust the piece of paper in Ethan's face.

"Rose C. was born with Down syndrome and a cleft palette. Her mother died at childbirth and her father, ashamed to be seen with his disfigured daughter, abandoned her. On her birthday one of the men from Covington found out where she was living, took pity on her, and asked her out on a date. My mother craved affection. She believed this man was genuine and loved her despite her physical condition. He promised to marry her. He even gave her an engagement ring. That night he took her to bed and had his way with her. After he shot his load he got up, dressed, and walked out of the house. She never saw him again. My mother died of a broken heart."

"You see," Jake's voice was shrill as he added, "I was never adopted! I was given to an orphanage by the Covingtons because I reminded them of my mother."

Scowling fiercely, Jake went nose to nose with Ethan: "I hated you the first day I met you. *Your* family loved *you*."

Ethan tried to change the subject, "Miriam and Luke adopted you."

Jake screamed, "How could they adopt me when Luke knew about my mother? I'll tell you why—he felt sorry for me!"

Suddenly in a single action, Jake ripped a revolver from his coat pocket.

Ethan's heart skipped a beat as he stared at the revolver. None of his training had prepared him for this. He thought of Margo and how alone she would be without him in her life.

Suddenly, Ethan realized that Jake wasn't pointing the revolver at him!

Jake put the barrel of the revolver to his own head.

Ethan collapsed to the living room floor as Jake's blood splattered everywhere.

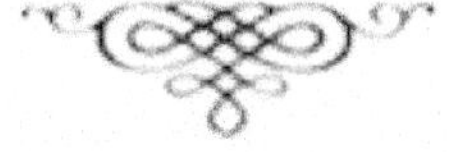

Chapter 25

A few days after Thanksgiving, Beulah sat in Graceland Park Cemetery on the wooden bench facing Sarah's and Andrew's grave markers. Old snow scrunched under the weight of her overshoes. She resembled a homeless woman dressed in layers of clothing, a blue knitted cap covered the top of her head.

She began her soliloquy, "*So much has happened in our lives since I was here last time. Where do I begin? I took Ethan to Ethel's fine jewelry to purchase a promise ring for him to give to Margo. The ring had five stones in it. The top stone was your birthday stone. The next two stones were for Ethan and Margo and the two bottom stones were for me and Tony. I told Ethan when he married Margo, he would give me his promise ring in exchange for his wedding ring. I gave Margo my engagement ring.*"

"*Margo and Ethan were married in Grace Episcopalian Church. The wedding was beautiful. Margo wore my wedding gown. The gown needed to be taken to a shop in town that does alternations so that my dress would fit her. Ethan wore his tuxedo. I purchased Ethan two wedding rings—one for him and the other for Margo. He was so handsome standing there in front of the church waiting for Margo to come into the sanctuary. Bud Silverman was his best man. Irene Silverman was Margo's matron of honor. I chose to take a seat in a pew in front of the church. I cried throughout the ceremony, knowing that you and Andrew were there sitting next to me."*

Beulah wiped the tears that began to flow down her cheeks. She clutched her handkerchief close to her side. *"Bud Silverman is the local Navy recruiter. He grew up on a farm south of here. One day his father was injured in a farming accident. The local doctor saved his father's life. It was then that Bud decided he wanted to be a doctor. His parents did not have the money to send Bud to medical school. Bud chose instead to enlist into the Navy when he graduated from high school. After he finished boot camp, he opted to become a Navy medic. Following basic training he applied to become a combat medic serving with the Marines."* Beulah was thoughtful for a moment and then she continued, *"Bud moved back here to be the Navy recruiter. He and Irene stayed at my place for a while until they bought a home in the area."*

"Ethan did not want to be drafted into the Army so he took the Navy's entrance examination. He scored in the 95th percentile. Bud asked Ethan what school he wanted to attend after he graduated from boot camp. Ethan told Bud that he wanted to attend medical school after basic and then he wanted to become a combat medic like Bud was. He had to obligate to five years' service if he wanted to be a combat medic like Bud. You would have been so proud to see Ethan in his Navy uniform. The Navy has given Ethan a sense of purpose in his life."

"Sarah, do you remember Jake Covington? He was an awful, screwed up boy that came into our lives after Miriam and Luke adopted him. He's dead now. He took his life one evening when he came to visit Ethan. Ethan

collapsed to the floor when Jake put a gun to his head and pulled the trigger. Blood splattered everywhere."

"Miriam went to live with her sister, Marsha, who lives in Fallon, Nevada. Miriam got a job at the officer's mess as a cashier and waitress. That's when she met Tyler Moore. Tyler flew jets for the Navy and after he retired, he went to work for an airline. Miriam called to me say that she had found her Andrew. I was happy for her. They were here for Thanksgiving, too."

Beulah stood as she stretched her arms above her head and that is when she noticed two robins perched on a tree limb.

She sobbed as she said, "I miss you both so much. Friends can be soul mates, too."

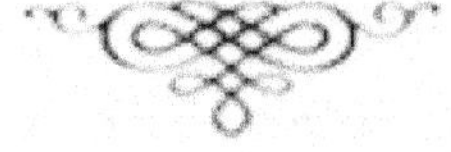

Acknowledgment

In 2017, I found Margaret Heisserer, my editor. I would never have completed this work without Margaret's suggestions.

www.ingramcontent.com/pod-product-compliance
Lightning Source LLC
Chambersburg PA
CBHW060600310726
48982CB00008B/1182/J

* 9 7 8 0 9 8 6 2 0 4 3 2 6 *